DOCTOR WHO AND THE
STONES OF BLOOD

Also available in the Target series:

DOCTOR WHO
AND THE
STONES OF BLOOD

Based on the BBC television serial by David Fisher by arrangement with the British Broadcasting Corporation

TERRANCE DICKS

A TARGET BOOK
published by
the Paperback Division of
W. H. Allen & Co. Ltd

A Target Book

Published in 1980
by the Paperback Division of W. H. Allen & CO. Ltd
A Howard & Wyndham Company
44 Hill Street, London W1X 8LB

Printed in Great Britain by
Richard Clay (The Chaucer Press) Ltd, Bungay, Suffolk

ISBN 0 426 20099 3

Contents

1

The Awakening of the Ogri

It might have been Stonehenge in the days of the Druids. A Circle of Stones stood in a hollow on the dark and lonely plain. Nine massive monoliths set in an irregular circle. One or two tilted, leaning, others still standing foursquare. Only three of the crosspieces were still in place, the others had crashed to the ground long centuries ago.

White-robed hooded figures were gathered in the circle, blazing torches in their hands. The fitful light flickered smokily on rapt, shadowed faces, reflected a red glare into glittering eyes.

A low, sonorous chant rose into the night air. 'Cailleach ... Cailleach ... Cailleach ...'

The chant rose higher. One of the hooded figures raised a long bronze horn and blew a deep throbbing note that shivered on the night air.

Two more hooded shapes came forward, each bearing a bronze bowl.

The bowls were filled with blood.

One of the fallen monoliths formed a kind of altar in the centre of the Circle. The bowls were placed reverently on this stone. Dark clouds scuddered windblown across the full moon. The chanting rose higher,

higher, *'Cailleach! Cailleach! Cailleach!'*

The robed figure of the High Priestess lifted one of the bowls and carried it to the nearest monolith. Carefully, she tipped the bowl so that the thick stream poured onto the stone.

The blood should have run straight down the side of the monolith ... it did not. Most of it was absorbed, as if swallowed by the stone. It was as though the stone itself was thirsty for blood. From deep within the monolith there was a fiery glow. A deep, throbbing groaning sound shuddered through the ground.

The High Priestess returned to the altar and lifted the second bowl. She carried it to another monolith, and poured again. The great stone soaked up the blood and glowed fierily in response. A throbbing groan like the note of some impossibly deep bell vibrated through the earth.

A great sigh of ecstasy went up from the worshipping circle.

The Priestess returned to the altar stone and stretched out her arms. Her high, clear voice rang through the circle. 'Come, oh great one, come. Your time is near!'

It might have been Stonehenge in the dark dawn of history.

The circle of stones was smaller, more compact.

The worshippers wore modern clothes beneath their robes.

But the forces upon which they were calling were more dark and dreadful than any summoned up by chanting Druids.

Fed by the warm blood they craved, the Ogri were awakening from their long sleep.

A police box which was not a police box at all sped through the space/time vortex. Inside it was an impossibly large control room with a many-sided central control console. Beside it stood a tall curly-haired man in a floppy broad-brimmed hat, and long trailing scarf, that mysterious traveller in time and space known as the Doctor. He had an irregularly-shaped crystal in his left hand, another in his right.

'Right, Doctor,' he said briskly to himself. 'Here we have two segments of the Key to Time. Just fit them together, and you can get on with finding number three.' He brought the two segments together. They wouldn't fit.

The Doctor frowned. Then his face cleared. 'Ah, I see, they go *this* way.' He tried again. They didn't.

Romana, the Doctor's Time Lady companion, came into the control room and stood watching him. 'Here, let me do it.'

'Just a minute, I can manage.' The Doctor tried again. He couldn't.

'I wish you'd let me help. I used to be rather good at puzzles.'

'Puzzles?' The Doctor was outraged. 'These are two segments of the Key to Time, possibly the most important object in the cosmos. You don't call that a mere puzzle, do you?'

'Well, no, not really.' Romana took the two crystals

9

from the Doctor's hands, studied them for a moment, then fitted them together. Immediately, they merged into an irregularly-shaped larger crystal, as if magnetised by some interior force. Romana handed the result back to the Doctor. 'There. Hardly complex enough to be called a puzzle, is it?'

'No, no,' said the Doctor, recovering rapidly. 'That was the trouble. It was just too simple for me!' He went over to a specially prepared wall-locker, opened it, put the crystal inside, closed it again. The locker was one of the most sophisticated wall safes in the universe and only the Doctor's personal palm print would re-open it.

'I gather that there are six of those segments to be found, Doctor, and so far we've only got two. Shouldn't we be getting a move on? Why don't you go and check our next destination?'

There were times when Romana's brisk bossiness infuriated the Doctor. 'This happens to be *my* TARDIS, I'll make the decisions here, if you don't mind.'

Romana gave him a withering look. 'Please yourself.'

'It just so happens I've decided to find out what our next destination will be,' said the Doctor with dignity.

Plugged into the central control console was a small, wandlike device called the Tracer. In conjunction with the TARDIS's instruments, the Tracer was supposed to determine the location in the universe of the next segment of the Key to Time. It could even lead them to the exact spot on the planet where the next crystal

10

could be found. At least, that was the idea.

The Doctor studied the instrument readings. 'Well, well, well! If my calculations are correct, there's a treat in store for you.'

'Really?' said Romana coldly. So far she hadn't been very impressed by the Doctor's predictions. 'Better than Calufrax, I hope?'

Calufrax was the last planet they had visited; Romana hadn't cared for it at all.

'Much better than Calufrax. You'll love it, Romana. I promise you you'll love it.'

'Really? If we *are* going to be arriving soon, I'd better change.'

She went out of the control room and the Doctor went back to studying his instruments.

Some time later, Romana came back into the control room. She was wearing a simple classical dress and a pair of extravagantly high-heeled shoes. 'Well, how do I look?'

The Doctor smiled, pleased to see that even Romana wasn't completely without vanity. 'Ravishing!'

'That's not what I meant, Doctor,' said Romana severely. 'I mean, will this outfit do for where we're going?'

'It'll do very nicely I should think—except for those shoes.'

Romana looked down. 'Oh, I rather like them.'

'Well, please yourself, I'm no fashion expert. But they don't look very practical.'

Romana sniffed and went out of the control room. Minutes later she came back, a pair of lower-heeled shoes in her hands. 'What about these, Doctor?'

Before the Doctor could reply, a deep mysterious voice boomed through the control room. 'Beware the Black Guardian!'

'What was that, Doctor? What does it mean?'

'It was by way of being a reminder—a warning to remember our mission and not waste time with fripperies.'

Hurriedly, Romana hung the shoes on the TARDIS hatstand. 'I wish I knew what you were talking about, Doctor. I've a feeling I don't really know what's going on.'

'If you were meant to know any more you'd have been told.'

'I *need* to know more about our mission, Doctor. After all, suppose something happened to you?'

'Something happen to me?' The Doctor considered. 'Well, perhaps you're right, it isn't really fair.'

'I should think it isn't! I was ordered to join you by the President of the Supreme Council of the Time Lords, told to help you in some mysterious mission . . .'

The Doctor sighed, wondering how he could explain *everything* to Romana. 'Well, for a start, you weren't sent on this mission by the President at all. The voice you just heard, and the being you saw in the shape of the President was the White Guardian. Or, to be more accurate, the Guardian of Light in Time. As opposed to the Guardian of Darkness sometimes called the Black Guardian. You've heard of the Guardians?'

Romana nodded, awestruck. Every Time Lord had heard of the Guardians though little was known about hem. They were two of the most powerful beings in he cosmos, infinitely more advanced than even the Time Lords.

'Then you know that they can assume any shape they wish? Well, so can the segments of the Key to Time.'

'But why was the Key divided in the first place?'

'The Key to Time is so powerful that it must never pass into the hands of one single being,' said the Doctor solemnly. 'That is why it was split up into six segments. These segments were disguised, and scattered throughout the universe.'

'If the segments are *supposed* to be split up, why are we doing our best to fit them together again?'

'Because there are times when the forces within the universe become so disturbed, the cosmic balance so badly upset, that the cosmos is in danger of being plunged into eternal chaos.'

Romana was beginning to understand. 'And the Key can prevent that from happening in some way?'

'When the Key is fully assembled and activated it can bring all Time to a stop. Then the White Guardian can restore the balance.'

'I see. And I suppose one of these times of cosmic imbalance is approaching?'

'Rapidly,' said the Doctor. 'That's why our mission is so terribly important ...'

A robot dog trundled into the control room and the Doctor bent down and patted it. 'Hello, K9!'

K9 had been the Doctor's companion on many adventures. In reality a fully mobile self-powered computer with defensive capabilities, he had been fashioned in

the shape of a dog by a space-station scientist who'
missed the pet he'd been forced to leave on Earth.

'Sensors indicate TARDIS landing imminen*
Master,' said K9 solemnly.

The Doctor looked at the TARDIS console. 'Righ*
as usual, K9. Get ready for your surprise, Roman*
We're landing!'

'Where?'

'Earth!'

'That's why you're looking so pleased. I might hav*
guessed, your favourite planet!'

'How do you know that?'

'Everybody knows that, Doctor.'

'They do?' said the Doctor puzzled. 'I don't remen*
ber telling everybody!'

'I can't think why you're so fond of the place.'

'I expect you'll like it too. It's pretty civilised on th*
whole.'

Romana studied the instruments that recorded e*
ternal conditions. 'Oxygen level seems acceptabl*
There seems to be some kind of liquid precipitatio*
though.'

'You mean it's raining?' The Doctor smiled. 'That*
because we've landed in England! It's what the loca*
call a nice day. Anyone for tennis?'

'Tennis?'

'An English expression. It means "Is anyone comin*
outdoors to get soaked".'

'Oh, I see,' said Romana, not seeing at all. She r*
moved the Tracer from the console and tucked it int*
her belt.

The Doctor went over to a wall locker, fished out a large umbrella, and opened the TARDIS door.

K9 trundled after him, but the Doctor said, 'Stay, K9. Guard duty for you, I'm afraid. We don't know if these particular natives are friendly yet.'

K9's tail antenna drooped despondently. 'Master.'

The Doctor went out, and Romana moved to follow him. She hesitated for a moment. 'K9, what is tennis?'

'Real, lawn or table, mistress?'

'Forget it!' said Romana and went out of the TARDIS.

K9 was puzzled, but he obeyed the instruction. 'Forget tennis! Erase information concerning tennis from memory banks. Memory erased!'

Outside the TARDIS, the Doctor and Romana were looking round. They were in the middle of a patch of rolling green moorland; there were trees and fields and the houses of what looked like a village to be seen in the distance. It was a soft and pleasant green landscape still wet with rain, though the rain had stopped now, and the returning sun was sending a hazy mist into the air.

The Doctor took a deep breath. 'I do believe it's going to be a nice day after all!'

Romana said, 'So this is Earth!' She didn't seem terribly impressed.

'Yes. Pretty isn't it?'

Romana had spent most of her life in the protected environment of the Time Lord Citadel on Gallifrey, and open countryside held few attractions for her. 'Well, we'd better get on with it.' She produced the Tracer and moved it in a circle. There was a sudden electronic buzz. 'It looks as if the third segment isn't far away. It must be over there.'

'Then let's go and find it!'

With that, the Doctor set off. Stumbling a little in her high-heeled shoes—she'd forgotten to change them after all—Romana followed him.

The Doctor led the way across the moor at a brisk pace, climbing a slight rise and descending the other side.

Suddenly, the Doctor stopped, knelt down, and examined the ground before him. 'That's very strange . . .'

'What is?'

'That is!' The Doctor pointed.

Stretching away across the moor ahead of them was a regularly-spaced series of deep round indentations.

They looked liked the footprints of some enormous beast.

2

The Circle of Power

Romana looked uneasily at the marks. 'What's so strange, Doctor? They're just marks, that's all, obviously caused by something very heavy.'

'Exactly,' said the Doctor, with sinister emphasis.

'Probably just some local animal ...'

'They don't have elephants in these parts, Romana. Whatever made the impressions must have weighed about three and a half tons.'

'Oh, more than that I should think,' said Romana confidently. She fitted one of her own feet into the nearest mark. 'Judging by the specific gravity of the ground round here, I'd say quite a bit more.'

The Doctor grunted. He didn't care for having his estimates challenged, even if they were largely guesswork.

Romana took out the Tracer and waved it about. There was another buzz. 'Over there!'

The Doctor followed the direction of Romana's gaze and saw a Circle of Stones looming on the horizon. 'That looks promising. Let's go and take a look.'

The Doctor dashed off without waiting for Romana. She hobbled after as quickly as she could in the impractical shoes. When she reached the circle the Doctor was wandering around inside it, examining the monoliths with keen scientific interest. 'What do you think of this then? Fascinating, eh?'

'Fascinating!' agreed Romana wearily. She sat down on the fallen stone in the centre of the circle and pulled off her shoes. 'What is this place anyway?'

'It's a stone circle.'

'I can see that. But what's it for?'

The Doctor, still absorbed, replied distractedly. 'It's a sort of megalithic temple observatory.'

'Observatory? But they're just stones—aren't they?'

'Just stones? Well, of course they're just stones. But they happen to be aligned with various points on the horizon, giving you sunrise and moonrise at different times of the year!'

'It all sounds terribly cumbersome. I didn't realise the people here were so primitive.'

'Primitive? I'm not talking about *now*. These things were set up thousands of years ago. In those days they were brilliant scientific achievements. Do you know, with some of these circles, they could even calculate eclipses.'

'Fascinating. Do you think one of these stones could be the third segment?'

The Doctor seemed more interested in the stone circle than in their mission. 'I don't know. Try the Tracer.'

Romana took out the Tracer and began passing it over the monoliths, one after the other. 'That's odd. There's nothing. Nothing at all!'

A voice from behind her said, 'It's all been surveyed, you know.'

Romana swung round. 'I beg your pardon?'

Behind her was a hooded figure—a woman in the kind of coat known on twentieth-century Earth as a duffle-coat.

The woman was quite old, though her back was straight, her eyes clear and alert. Her straggly hair was a snowy white, her face a mass of lines and wrinkles. It was the face of a woman of formidable character. 'I said the circle has been surveyed—many times.'

Romana didn't have the slightest idea what the old lady was talking about.

The Doctor didn't either, but he nodded wisely and said, 'Ah, quite!'

'May I ask what you're doing here then?'

'Well, that's a bit tricky, actually. You might say we're conducting an investigation.'

'Aha! So you noticed it too, then?'

'Well . . .' said the Doctor modestly.

'I knew it was only a matter of time before some other academic noticed the discrepancies.' She grabbed the Doctor's hand and shook it vigorously. 'Haven't we met somewhere before?' She peered into his face. 'Now let me see, you're Professor . . . ?'

'Doctor actually.'

'Ah, yes, Doctor . . . Now don't tell me, I've a wonderful memory for faces. Doctor . . . Doctor Fougous!'

'Fougous?' said the Doctor unenthusiastically. It might be useful to have a new name for a while, but

19

he didn't much care for the sound of this one.

'Fougous!' said the old lady decidedly. 'I'd kno
you anywhere. Doctor Cornish Fougous. You gave
lecture at that archaeological conference at Princeto
—or was it Cardiff?'

'I'm afraid I don't quite recall ...'

'Perhaps it was that fool Leamington-Smythe wh
gave it then?' She glared fiercely at him. 'Anyway,
was a dreadful lecture. Complete bosh.'

The Doctor was beginning to feel rather ove
whelmed—an unusual sensation for him. 'Well, tha
seems to take care of me! Now may I ask who you ar
Madam?'

'I am Professor Amelia Rumford,' said the old lad
grandly. She looked at the Doctor, obviously expectin
a reaction. When he didn't say anything, she adde
rather plaintively. 'The authoress of *Bronze Ag
Burials in Gloucestershire*, you know!'

The Doctor swept off his hat and gave her one of h
most charming smiles. 'Yes, of course! The definitiv
work on the subject, if I may say so!'

Professor Rumford smiled, and almost blushe
'You're too kind, Doctor—but you're quite right
Her face turned shrewd again, and she gave him a
appraising look. 'I suppose it was Doctor Borlase
survey of 1754 that put you on to it?'

'Well ...' said the Doctor vaguely. 'Amongst othe
things ...'

Professor Amelia Rumford rattled on. 'That's ho
I first twigged, when I came to compare Doctor Bo
lase's work with the Reverend Thomas Bright's surve

f 1820. And when I checked up on the two surveys of 876 and 1911, well, it was obvious, wasn't it?'

Romana was completely baffled by now. 'What was obvious?'

The Doctor realised he hadn't made the proper introductions. 'Forgive me, Professor Rumford. This is my assistant, Romana.'

Professor Rumford grabbed Romana's hand and shook it heartily. 'How do you do, my dear? Charming name, Romana. Never heard it before? What's its origin I wonder?'

Romana decided they'd better not go into that. She repeated her question. 'What was obvious?'

'Either they were miscounted or ...'

'What was miscounted?'

'The stones. The Nine Travellers here.' The old lady waved her hand around the stone circle. 'It's the local name for them.'

Romana looked round. 'That seems logical. There are nine of them!'

Professor Rumford's leathery old face cracked into a rather sinister smile. 'Yes. But in earlier surveys they were sometimes called the Six Travellers, or the Seven Travellers. It's as if the stones could *move*. Odd isn't it?'

The Doctor noticed several dark patches on the ground, near the base of one of the stones. 'So is this, Professor.'

'What is?'

The Doctor straightened up. 'Dried blood. None on the stone, but quite a lot of it here on the ground, as if something had had its throat cut.'

'Something probably did!'

The Doctor whirled round. A tall, black-hooded figure had entered the Circle of Stones. Momentarily it looked utterly sinister. A closer look revealed a tall strikingly attractive dark-haired woman in her forties wearing a kind of hooded cloak.

Professor Rumford said, 'Ah, there you are, Vivien! Doctor, this is my friend Vivien Fay. This is the Doctor Vivien, and this is his assistant, Miss Romana.'

There was an exchange of polite 'Hello's.'

The Doctor said, 'You move very quietly, Miss Fay. I didn't hear you approach.'

'I used to be a Brown Owl.'

'Oh, really,' said Romana wondering if the people of this peculiar planet had the power to change into birds.

'She means the leader of a Brownie Pack,' explained the Doctor. 'It's an organisation for little girls—oh never mind!' He turned back to Miss Fay. 'What about this spilled blood then? It doesn't bother you at all.'

'Oh, it's probably just the remains of another sacrifice!'

Romana looked at the Doctor. 'I thought you told me the Earth was civilised by now?'

'Sssh,' said the Doctor warningly. 'There have been sacrifices before then, Miss Fay?'

'I'm afraid so, the BIDS tend to be a bit primitive in their rituals.'

'The BIDS?'

'The British Institute of Druidic Studies. Nothing to do with any real druids of course, past or present. It's a rather strange little group who come here regularly. They dress up in white robes and wave bits of mistletoe and curved knives in the air. It's all very stagey and unhistoric.'

Professor Rumford frowned. 'I think you may be dismissing them a little too lightly, Vivien. I'm not convinced they're as harmless as you make out.'

'Why?' asked the Doctor swiftly. 'Has there been trouble?'

'Yes, there has as a matter of fact. I've had several brushes with their leader, a Mr De Vries. A most inpleasant man!'

'Really?'

Miss Fay said, 'I took you for one of his group at first, Doctor. As I said, they tend to be a little eccentric.' She looked pointedly at the Doctor's floppy hat and trailing scarf.

The Doctor seemed quite untroubled. 'I take it you don't have very much to do with these people then?'

'No more than we can help,' said Professor Rumford spiritedly. 'All that mumbo jumbo and antiquated nonsense. Vivien and I are conducting a piece of genuine scholastic research. We're doing a complete topographical, geological, astronomical and archeological survey of the site!'

'Good for you,' said the Doctor absently. 'Tell me, where can I find this Mr De Vries?'

'He lives in the big house, over there.' She pointed to a path leading over the hill ahead of them.

The Doctor nodded thoughtfully. 'You know, I think I might go and look him up.'

'What now, Doctor?' hissed Romana. She nodded meaningly at the stones. Surely they should be getting on with their quest?

'Yes, now,' said the Doctor firmly.

'I warn you, he doesn't much care for scientists,' said Professor Rumford.

'Very few people do, in my experience,' said the Doctor ruefully. 'Oh by the way, we saw some rather strange indentations on the ground on our way here. Back over there.'

'Yes,' said Miss Fay. 'I noticed them too. Probably one of the local farmers moving heavy equipment.'

'Very probably.' The Doctor turned to Professor Rumford. 'Mr De Vries's house is over there, you say?'

'That's right. You can't miss it.'

'How far is it?'

'Oh, can't be more than a couple of miles.'

It was obvious that a mile or two was nothing to Professor Rumford. Romana felt very differently. 'A couple of miles?' She looked down at her feet.

'I warned you about those shoes,' said the Doctor severely.

'Yes, Doctor, I know you did.'

Professor Rumford looked at her own stout brogues and then at Romana's shoes. 'See what you mean. Not very practical for a field trip are they?'

'I didn't realise we would be going hiking, Doctor.'

The Doctor smiled infuriatingly. 'She wouldn't be told, Professor. Still there you are. Look, tell you what

Romana, why don't you stay on here with these two ladies? I'll stop off on my way back and pick up some comfortable boots for you. All right?'

Romana sighed resignedly. 'All right.' She didn't much fancy the idea, but it was better than slogging across the moor in high-heeled shoes.

The Doctor moved closer to her. 'Listen, keep an eye on things while you're here—and keep an eye on those two. I've got a feeling there's something very odd going on!'

Romana nodded.

The Doctor moved away. 'Well, cheerio, then,' he said loudly. 'I shan't be long. Goodbye, ladies.'

The Doctor raised his hat and strode away. Soon he was climbing the path with rapid strides, his long scarf trailing behind him.

Miss Fay looked disapprovingly after his retreating figure. 'A typical piece of male behaviour. Strands you here in the middle of nowhere, while he goes off enjoying himself. Fancy leaving you with two complete strangers. Why we might be anybody!'

'Never mind,' said Professor Rumford consolingly. She had recognised a fellow spirit in the Doctor. Once something engaged his interest, he just had to be off in pursuit of it. 'As long as you're here, Romana, perhaps you'd like to help us with the survey?'

Not far away, the Doctor was kneeling by yet another deep indentation in the ground. Whatever it was had moved over in this direction too. He straightened up.

'Farm machinery indeed! Ha!'

From somewhere overhead, a derisive cawing seemed to echo his remark.

The Doctor looked up. A flock of big black birds circled overhead. Rooks, or crows, probably thought the Doctor.

He set off down the path. Glancing up again, he saw the birds keeping pace with him.

It was almost as if they were following him.

3

De Vries

Romana held one end of the measuring tape, while Amelia Rumford stretched it across to the next stone. 'Sure you've got it straight?' she puffed. 'Jolly good. What is it now ... Twenty-eight point nine metres.' She noted it down in her book. 'Jolly good, girls. Let's have a breather now. Take five, as they say.' She produced the rather dated Americanism with conscious pride.

Romana straightened up, releasing her end of the tape. A sudden loud cawing sound made her jump. A big black bird was perched on the stone above her head. Romana jumped back. 'What's that?'

Miss Fay gave one of her acid smiles. 'Nothing to be afraid of—it's only a crow.'

Romana shuddered. 'Ugh! It looks—evil, somehow.'

From its perch on top of the monolith, the crow stared balefully down at her.

In De Vries's big house on the hill, that house to which the Doctor was even now making his way, there was a room with white-washed walls, a stone floor, and a ceiling supported by great oak beams, blackened with

27

age. A curtained alcove at the back of the room was furnished as a kind of temple. There were silken drapes decorated with strange cabalistic signs. An altar stood at the back of the alcove, two white-robed figures beside it.

On the altar stood a kind of brazier. One of the robed figures was De Vries himself. He raised his hand and the brazier burst into flame. Thick incense laden smoke drifted above the altar.

De Vries began to chant. 'Cailleach, Cailleach, Cailleach, Great Goddess. We are here to do your bidding!'

The second robed figure took up the chant. This was Martha, High Priestess of the cult. 'Oh, Cailleach, Cailleach, Cailleach.'

There was a sudden flurry of wings and a great, black bird came to perch on a stand before the altar.

'Oh Cailleach, your spirit fills us,' chanted De Vries. 'Your worshippers are our brothers, your enemies are our enemies. Death to the enemies of the Cailleach!'

Martha echoed the chant. 'Death to the enemies of the Cailleach.'

De Vries picked up the curved knife that lay on the altar and raised it high.

Swinging his umbrella jauntily, the Doctor strode up to the gates of the old dark house. It was a forbidding mansion with a gothic, castle-like appearance, its chimneys dark against the evening sky. There were crows perching on those chimneys. The Doctor studied the brass plate on the gatepost. On it was engraved 'De

Vries'. He went up the long gravel drive, flanked by rows of dank shrubbery, onto the arched stone porch, and rang the bell set beside the huge oak door.

The bell clanged through the corridors of the old house, penetrating as far as the altar room.

'He comes, oh Cailleach,' chanted De Vries. 'The one whose coming was foretold is here! Your will shall be obeyed, oh Cailleach.' He laid the curved knife back upon the altar, and set a metal lid upon the brazier, extinguishing the flame. He slipped off his robe and handed it to Martha, revealing himself as a dapper-looking man with a rather Continental appearance.

As he opened the altar room door the bell pealed again. From the front doorstep a voice could be heard calling, 'Hello there! Anybody in!'

De Vries smiled. 'Our guest is impatient. We must not keep him waiting.' He gave a final glance in the mirror, straightened his tie, and made for the front door.

The Doctor got bored with ringing the bell. On impulse, he tried the front door. To his surprise, it opened, and since the Doctor was, as always, insatiably curious, he went inside.

He found himself in a long dark hallway lined with paintings, 'Hello. Anyone at home?'

Silence. 'Nobody here but us Druids,' murmured the

Doctor and wandered down the hall, studying the paintings. They were all portraits, a seventeenth-century priest, a man in eighteenth-century dress, a woman in the costume of the early nineteenth century. But there was a gap in the row of portraits, or rather three gaps. Three rectangular patches of lighter wallpaper showed that three portraits had been removed.

The Doctor wandered up to the portrait of the eighteenth-century priest. He read the little plaque beneath the painting. 'Doctor Thomas Borlase, 1701–1754. So that's the good Doctor! '

'He surveyed the Travellers, you know,' said a voice behind him. 'But then you probably know that already, Doctor.'

The Doctor turned. 'Mr De Vries?'

'That is correct.'

'How did you know my name?'

The man came to stand beside the Doctor. 'It was very sad about Doctor Borlase, you know.'

'Really? What happened to him?'

'Didn't Professor Rumford tell you?'

'No, I don't believe she did.'

'One of the Circle stones fell on him—just after he completed his survey.'

'Maybe we should warn Professor Rumford?'

'Oh no, no, no, *I'm* sure she'll be quite safe.'

The Doctor indicated the three squares of lighter wallpaper. 'What happened to those pictures?'

'They're all away, being cleaned. One of them's rather fine actually, by that Scottish painter, Ramsey.

It's a portrait of Lady Montcalm—perhaps you've heard of her?'

'No, I'm afraid not.'

'The Montcalm family used to own this house,' said De Vries, with a kind of sinister emphasis. 'The house and most of the surrounding area—including the Nine Travellers. They called her the Wicked Lady Montcalm, you know. She was said to have murdered her husband on their wedding night.' De Vries pointed to the next space. 'That was a portrait of a Mrs Trefusis. Something of a recluse. She lived here for nearly six years and never saw a soul.' He indicated the third space. 'And that's a Brazilian lady, or it would be if it was there. Senhora Camara.'

'Was there a Senhor Camara?' asked the Doctor idly.

'If there was he doesn't seem to have survived the crossing from Brazil.' De Vries broke off. 'But why are we standing about in the hall? Let me offer you a glass of sherry.'

'How very hospitable of you,' said the Doctor urbanely. 'Yes, I should like that very much ...'

The measuring was completed for the day, and Professor Amelia Rumford was gathering up her equipment, stowing theodolite, marking stakes, tape measures, and a clutter of other equipment in a big wicker workbox.

Romana looked up. 'Those crows are still there. They've been circling around us all afternoon.'

The old lady nodded absently, not really taking in

what Romana was saying. 'Well, that's it for the day, I think. Thank you for all your help, Romana. Fancy coming back for a mug of tea and some sandwiches?'

Miss Fay reinforced the invitation. 'Please do. My cottage is really very close.'

Romana was tempted, but she shook her head. 'I'd better wait for the Doctor. If I leave here, he won't know where I am.'

'Oh well, please yourself,' said Professor Rumford gruffly. 'Still, if you do change your mind, we're not far away.' She pointed. 'Just over there.'

'Yes, do come,' said Miss Fay, sweetly. 'Bring your friend with you, when he gets back.'

'All right,' said Romana. 'We'll come if we can.'

'Good. We'll hope to see you later then.' Miss Fay and Professor Rumford moved off.

Left alone in the circle at last, Romana was able to go on with her own survey—the quest for the third segment of the Key to Time. She took out the Tracer, and scanned stone after stone—without the slightest result.

Romana shook her head, completely baffled.

She heard a derisive cawing sound and looked up.

Above her the crows were still circling endlessly.

In the altar room the curtains were drawn across the alcove, concealing the altar. They gave the room a rather odd look, like a theatre before the performance.

The Doctor was admiring the crow which was perched on the stand in front of the curtains. 'That's a pretty unusual pet, isn't it?'

De Vries handed him a glass of sherry. 'It isn't exactly what you'd call a pet, Doctor. Do sit down.'

The Doctor sank down into an armchair. 'No? You know, you never did tell me how you knew my name.'

De Vries took a chair opposite the Doctor. 'Didn't I, Doctor? But then you never told me the reason for your interest in the Circle.'

'Well, as a matter of fact, I'm looking for something.'

'What?'

'A key,' said the Doctor solemnly. 'Or to be exact, part of a key!'

'A key to what?'

The Doctor gestured vaguely with his free hand. 'Oh, just a key. It seems to have been mislaid. Tell me, Mr De Vries, you're not really a Druid, are you?'

'Well, not in the conventional sense no. But in my humble way I am a keen student of Druidic lore.'

'That must be terribly boring,' said the Doctor politely.

It was a moment before De Vries realised what the Doctor had actually said. He sat bolt upright in his chair, quivering with rage. 'Boring? What do you mean, boring?'

'Well,' said the Doctor easily, 'there's not really very much to know about the Druids is there? Not that's historically reliable, I mean. Oh, there's the odd mention in Julius Caesar's memoirs, a line or two in Tacitus.' The Doctor mentioned the names of these two Ancient Romans as though they were old friends, as indeed they were. He'd always got on very well with

Julius Caesar, though you couldn't really trust him. And, of course, he'd never listen to advice. Even when the Doctor had gone to all the trouble of dressing up as a soothsayer, and croaking 'Beware the Ides of March', old Julius wouldn't listen.

The Doctor realised his thoughts were wandering, and came back to the angry little man in the chair before him. He decided to provoke him a little further. When people became angry they were indiscreet, and that's when you learned something.

He took a sip of his sherry. 'You know,' he said conversationally, 'I always thought Druids were more or less invented by old John Aubrey, back in the seventeenth century, as a sort of joke. He loved a joke, old John.'

Aubrey was a famous diarist, who had published a long rambling work full of scandalous stories about the famous people of his day. De Vries was furious at having his sacred Druidism associated with what he regarded as a deplorable old scandal monger.

'This is no laughing matter, Doctor!'

The Doctor yawned. 'That's a pity, I enjoy a laugh. Well, come on then, what's your interest in the Stones?'

'The Stones are sacred,' said De Vries, in a hushed voice.

The Doctor seemed unimpressed. 'Sacred to whom?'

'To one who is mighty and all powerful. To the Goddess.'

'Goddess?' said the Doctor sceptically. 'What Goddess is that?'

'She has many names. Morriga ... Hermentana ... but those who serve her today call her the Cailleach.'

'The Cailleach,' repeated the Doctor thoughtfully. 'So your Goddess is Celtic in origin, then?'

De Vries's voice was hushed and reverent. 'She is the Goddess of War ... of Death ... of Magic!'

The Doctor rose and stretched out a finger to stroke the glossy black head of the crow. It pecked viciously at him, and he snatched his hand away just in time.

De Vries smiled. 'Beware of the crow and the raven, Doctor. They are the eyes of the Cailleach.'

The Doctor turned. 'You don't really believe all that stuff, do you?'

'I believe, Doctor. I believe because I have seen her power. Come.'

De Vries rose and crossed to the curtains. He pulled a silken cord, drawing them back with a flourish.

Standing behind the altar was a truly terrifying figure, white robed with a feathered bird-mask covering the face. A female figure, with a feathered face that looked incredibly cruel and evil, but more than that it radiated power.

The Doctor stared, fascinated. He heard swift movement behind him, half turned—and caught a fleeting glimpse of De Vries, a heavy copper bowl raised high above his head.

The bowl came crashing down, and everything went black ...

The bird-masked figure seemed to float from behind the altar. She stooped beside the Doctor and reached out a taloned hand, touching a vein that pulsed in the Doctor's neck.

In a trembling voice De Vries said, 'His blood is still warm, O Cailleach! I know what I must do.'

The Cailleach rose. The cruel eyes behind the bird-mask widened, and glinted malevolently as they stared into the distance.

It was becoming dark inside the Circle of Stones. There was no sound except the rustle of the wind in the nearby trees, and the occasional cawing of the crows.

Romana paced uneasily to and fro, wishing the Doctor would return. She sensed rather than heard movement behind her, and whirled round. Her eyes widened. 'Doctor? Where have you been?'

She stared into the dusk. 'Doctor, are you all right? You want me to come with you?'

Kicking off her useless shoes, Romana began walking across the circle as if drawn by some invisible force.

The compulsion led her across the moor, through the trees and along a rutted path that ended at the top of a cliff.

Romana walked slowly to the very edge of the cliff and looked down. Far below the sea was pounding on jagged rocks.

She turned. 'What is it, Doctor? Why have you brought me here?'

She backed away. 'Doctor, what's the matter? Hey.' Her eyes widened and she screamed, 'No! Doctor no!'

She took another step backward—into nothingness.

esperately she tried to recover her balance but it was
oo late. With a scream of terror, she pitched over the
dge of the cliff.

4

The Sacrifice

Arms and legs flailing wildly, Romana fell ... Her
hands grabbed a bush, growing from the side of the
cliff. It pulled away, but her fall was slowed a little
and the next bush she caught hold of held, though she
could feel it beginning to loosen ...

Her bare feet scrabbled desperately against the rock
face below her, feeling for a hold ... and she managed
to get the toes of first one foot and then the other into
a crevice of rock. Cautiously, she put as much of her
weight on them as she dared, in an effort to take the
strain from the little bush she was clutching.

Clinging precariously to the cliff face by fingers and
toes, Romana threw back her head and screamed,
'Help! Please, someone help me!'

The only answer was the crashing of the waves on
the rocks far below.

The Doctor, the real Doctor, not the false shape that
had lured Romana into such danger, was stretched
out unconscious on the fallen altar-stone in the Circle.

A semi-circle of robed figures were grouped around
him, De Vries in the centre. 'Bind him to the Stone,

rdered De Vries. Two robed acolytes hurried to obey.

Carefully, De Vries put a bronze bowl on the stone
eside the Doctor's head.

Another robed figure approached. It was Martha,
he High Priestess. 'I don't like it! You're not really
oing through with this?'

De Vries's face was rapt, his voice a hypnotised
rone. 'It is the will of the Goddess.'

'It's murder!'

'We may not oppose the Goddess's will.'

'Think,' urged Martha. 'Think what you're doing!'

'The Cailleach demands blood.'

'She's never demanded human sacrifices before.'

De Vries looked anguishedly at her. 'I dare not
ppose her will, Martha. I dare not.'

'If it is her will, why isn't she here?'

'She will come. The Cailleach will come.'

'This man may be missed. He'll have friends, they'll
ell the police . . .' Martha was close to panic. She was
local schoolteacher, and she had joined the cult be-
ause of her friendship with De Vries, and because the
Druid rituals and sacrifices brought some colour into
very dull life. But she was no criminal, and she had
ever expected to be faced with cold-blooded murder.

De Vries was too far under the influence of the Cail-
each to be reached by reason. 'He will not be missed.
The Cailleach will have foreseen everything. We must
ave faith. She will come.'

De Vries lifted the great curved knife from the altar
nd leaned over the Doctor's recumbent form.

At this point the Doctor rather spoiled the solemnity

of the occasion by opening his eyes. 'Hello!'

Martha gave a scream and jumped back.

The Doctor looked at the gleaming knife, inches from his throat. 'I hope that knife's been properly sterilised!'

'Blasphemer!' hissed De Vries.

'No, no, no,' protested the Doctor. 'You can catch all sorts of nasty things from a dirty knife, you know. There's tetanus, commonly known as lockjaw, not to mention a whole variety of staphylococcal infections.'

Suddenly, Martha realised that it was quite impossible to kill the Doctor now. It had been bad enough when he was unconscious, but now he was alive, and talking ... She stepped back. 'I'm having nothing more to do with this.'

'Good for you!' said the Doctor warmly.

De Vries was undeterred. 'That is not important. I will do what must be done.'

'Tell me does your Cailleach ride a rather ancient bicycle?' asked the Doctor.

'You will die with blasphemy on your lips,' hissed De Vries.

'It's just that I can see someone on an old bike coming this way, if I'm not mistaken.' The Doctor raised his voice and bellowed. 'Hey! Over here!'

The robed figures looked round in alarm.

A figure on a bicycle was pedalling furiously towards them. It was Professor Amelia Rumford.

'Help! Help! Over here!' yelled the Doctor lustily. In a high cracked voice Professor Rumford creeched, 'I'm coming! I'm coming! Hang on!'

The arrival of the newcomer was enough to break the spell. De Vries snatched up the knife and bowl and fled. The others followed him. Soon the Doctor was left alone stretched out on his stone. He gave a great sigh of relief. It had been a near thing, but he had made it.

By the time Professor Rumford wobbled to a halt beside the altar stone, the Circle was empty.

She dismounted, propped her heavy old-fashioned bicycle against the nearest monolith, and looked down at the Doctor. 'Good grief, man, what do you think you're doing? You'll catch your death of cold.'

The Doctor grinned. 'You know how it is Professor. I often get all tied up in my work!'

Professor Rumford produced a serviceable-looking clasp-knife and began cutting through the cords that bound the Doctor to the stone. 'What were those people up to? Some of that Druid lot, weren't they? Looked as if they were going to cut your throat!'

'I don't think they'd *quite* made up their minds, but that was definitely one of their options! What brought you back here?'

Professor Rumford tapped the basket on the handle-bars of her bike. 'I came back to bring that poor 'gel' Romana some sandwiches and a thermos of tea. I know how irresponsible you men are. I thought she'd still be waiting here for you.'

The last of the cords fell away and the Doctor sat up, flexing his cramped limbs. 'I thought she was with you?'

'No, she insisted on staying behind here to wait for you.'

The Doctor stood up and looked round worriedly. 'Then where is she?' He threw back his head and yelled. 'Romana! Romana! Romana, where are you?'

His voice echoed eerily around the stones, but there was no other reply. 'Nothing! And she could have gone off in any direction.'

'I don't want to be an alarmist,' said Professor Rumford. 'But we're quite near the coast here and there are some very sheer cliffs ... There are old mine shafts on the moor, too. It can be very dangerous in the dark.'

'Oh thanks a lot,' said the Doctor bitterly. He noticed a couple of objects lying on the ground. He picked them up, and held them out to Professor Rumford. 'Well here are her shoes, anyway.'

'Well,' said Professor Rumford philosophically, 'the only thing we can do is wait till morning, and organise a proper search.' She looked at the shoes. 'Now, if only we had a dog, preferably a bloodhound, we could give him the shoes and ...'

'A dog?' shouted the Doctor. 'Well, of course, we've got a dog! Professor Rumford, may I call you Amelia by the way, you are a genius!'

The old lady stared at him. 'You *do* have a dog?'

'A dog? Have I got a dog!' said the Doctor exultantly. He fished a whistle-like object from his pocket and blew hard, though no sound emerged.

'Oh, I see,' said Professor Rumford. 'That's one of those soundless high-frequency dog whistles, isn't it? So high-pitched we can't hear them, but dogs can?'

42

'Yes, something like that,' said the Doctor vaguely. He put the whistle to his lips and blew again. 'Come on K9. Wake up!'

Inside the TARDIS K9 stirred. He had been resting, dormant, conserving his energy-resources as was his habit when not needed. Now as the Doctor's high frequency signal stimulated his auditory circuits, he came to life. His eye-screens lit up, his tail antenna quivered.

'Master?' said K9. 'Master?' He glided towards the TARDIS doors, sending out a remote-control energy-impulse that caused the doors to open before him.

Outside the TARDIS, K9 swivelled to and fro for a moment, trying to fix the direction from which the signal was coming. Once this was established, he set off into the night.

The Doctor turned to Professor Rumford, 'Look, I'll get out and try to meet my dog halfway. The sooner we get him started tracking the better. You stay here in case Romana happens to come back.'

'Very well, Doctor.' She smiled at him with positively girlish enthusiasm. 'I say, this is all getting rather exciting, isn't it?'

'Let's hope it doesn't get too exciting,' said the Doctor and set off across the moor.

He hurried in the direction of the TARDIS as fast as he could, and soon encountered K9 gliding down the path. In fact K9 was shooting along so fast the

Doctor nearly fell over him. 'There you are K9! Wh
can't you bark or something?'

'I am not programmed for canine vocal effects
Master.'

'Never mind. Listen, you've always wanted to be
bloodhound, haven't you?'

'Negative, Master,' said K9, who was quite satisfie
with being an automaton.

'Yes you have,' said the Doctor. 'Well, here's you
chance. Find Romana.'

K9 whirred and clicked. 'Programme activated
Master. Mistresses's scent, blood and tissue type, an
alphawave brain pattern are all recoded in my dat
bank.'

'Don't just talk about it, K9. Do it!'

K9 spun round in a slow circle, stopped and the
swung back again. 'Getting direction, Master . . . I hav
direction—now!'

'Good dog, K9. Good dog! Off you go then!'

K9 glided away across the moor, and the Docto
followed.

Like a lizard on a wall, Romana clung desperately t
the crumbling cliff face. She kept finding new hand
holds, new crevices for her toes, but always after
time she felt her grip beginning to slip.

She dared not look down at the jagged rocks belo
and instead stared fixedly at the cliff-edge above her
so near and yet so impossible to reach. She ha

screamed for help until she was hoarse, but no one had come.

Suddenly she saw a familiar dog-like head project above the line of the cliff-top. A voice called, 'Mistress?'

'K9! Am I pleased to see you! I was so frightened!'

'Fear is unnecessary, Mistress. The Doctor is with me. We shall rescue you.'

'The Doctor?' gasped Romana. 'Oh, no!'

The Doctor heard the voice from below him, and was understandably hurt. 'Romana, where are you? What's the matter?'

'Keep away!' screamed Romana. 'Keep away from me!'

'What's the matter with you?'

'Watch him, K9. Keep him off of me!'

The Doctor unwound his scarf and dangled it over the edge of the cliff. 'Listen, stop messing about down here, will you? Grab hold of this.'

'Oh no,' called Romana. 'I'm not giving you a second chance. It was you who shoved me over the edge!'

'Me?' protested the Doctor. 'Never! Come on, grab hold.'

Reluctantly, Romana caught hold of the dangling scarf and the Doctor drew her upwards.

She scrambled up over the cliff edge, and backed rapidly away from him. 'Get away from me!'

'What's the matter, Romana?'

'You pushed me! You pushed me over the cliff!'

'Whatever pushed you, Romana, it wasn't me.'

45

'Then how do I know you're really the Doctor?' demanded Romana hysterically.

The Doctor sighed, 'K9, who am I?'

There was rather a disturbing silence.

'Well, come on, K9. Who am I? Tell her who I am!'

'Kindly do not interrupt, Master. Scanning process in operation ... cross-checking data ...' K9 whirred and buzzed. 'You are the Doctor, Master.'

The Doctor looked triumphantly at Romana. 'There you are. I am the Doctor! I knew I was.'

'Well, if *you* didn't push me over, what did? It was no thought projection, believe me. It was solid!'

'And it looked exactly like me?'

'The image of you ...' Romana caught her breath. 'Doctor—the third segment. It has the power to transform objects, or at least their appearances. Someone's got hold of it, and they've found a way of utilising its powers.'

'Yes,' said the Doctor slowly. 'I think you're right.'

'What are we going to do about it, then?'

'We can start by getting you a decent pair of shoes!'

They made their way back across the moor and into the TARDIS, where Romana hurried to her quarters and changed into warmer clothing and a pair of sensible shoes. When she emerged the Doctor was pacing thoughtfully up and down the control room, watched by K9. He looked up. 'Better now?'

'Yes, thanks.'

'Good. You've still got the Tracer?'

'Yes, of course I have.' Romana tapped the slender

46

wand-like device in her belt.

'Good. I want you to check the Circle of Stones again.'

Romana looked indignantly at him. 'What do you think I was doing when you—well, when *something,* lured me to that cliff top and pulled me off? There was no trace of the segment, I promise you.'

'Well, it's got to be somewhere, hasn't it?'

'Well, it can't be there and not there at the same time,' said Romana exasperatedly.

'Of course it can! How's your interspatial geometry?'

'Pretty rusty,' admitted Romana. 'And I don't see how interspatial geometry can explain——'

'Good, good,' said the Doctor cheerfully. 'Come on then, let's go!' He hurried out.

Romana looked down at K9. 'Do you understand? How can a thing be in one place and yet not be in that place?'

K9's only reply was an electronic burble as he tried to compute the problem.

'If you mean you don't know, why don't you just say so?' demanded Romana crossly.

She followed the Doctor out of the TARDIS and K9 glided after her.

They made their way across the darkened moor, back to the Circle of Stones.

5

The Ogri Attack

Huddled inside her duffle-coat, Professor Amelia Rumford paced up and down the darkened Circle of Stones. 'I shouldn't have let the Doctor go off on his own. I shouldn't have let him go at all! He doesn't know the moor, he doesn't understand the dangers.'

Cloaked and hooded, Miss Fay sat calm and relaxed on the altar stone. 'Amelia, you mustn't blame yourself.'

'I should have gone to search for the girl myself!'

'Someone had to stay here in case the girl came back,' Miss Fay reminded her.

'Then it should have been the Doctor!'

Had Professor Rumford but known, the Doctor and Romana (and of course K9) weren't far away. They were on the moor, just outside the Circle. Romana had the Tracer in her hand.

'Go on,' said the Doctor encouragingly. 'Try again!' Romana tried, and the high-pitched electronic note showed that the third segment was bafflingly close.

'You hear that?' asked Romana. 'Positive. Definitely positive!'

The Doctor smiled enigmatically. 'Yes, that's exactly what I expected. Come on!'

He led the way towards the Circle of Stones.

When they arrived, Miss Fay was still reassuring the agitated Professor Rumford. 'You mustn't worry so, Amelia. I'm sure the Doctor is perfectly capable of looking after himself!'

'I'm not so sure of that!' called Romana.

Professor Rumford turned. 'Oh, there you are! You're safe! And Romana's safe as well!'

'Of course we are,' said the Doctor.

K9 glided forward, and the old lady jumped back in astonishment. 'Good heavens, what's that?'

'This is my dog, Professor. He's called K9. He found Romana for us—didn't you K9?'

'Affirmative, Master.'

'But he's—mechanical,' said Professor Rumford in astonishment.

'Affirmative,' said K9 smugly.

'Isn't that rather unusual?'

'Manufactured in Trenton, New Jersey,' explained the Doctor hurriedly. 'They're all the rage in America.'

Professor Rumford was relieved. She could accept anything, however unusual, if it came from America. 'Oh really? Tell me, do you have to have a licence for it?'

'Negative,' said K9, determined to show he could answer for himself.

'Er, no,' confirmed the Doctor. 'No you don't.'

Romana produced the Tracer and began scanning the area.

The high-pitched electronic buzz made Miss Fa
jump. 'What's that?'

'Oh, just another little gadget,' said the Doctor hur
riedly.

Romana looked at him, 'You see Doctor? It's *here*
It's definitely *here*.'

The Doctor nodded. 'Yes, it's here all right—some
where!'

'What is?' asked Miss Fay curiously.

No one answered her question.

'I still don't understand,' said Romana.

The Doctor rubbed his chin. 'Don't you? I think
I'm beginning to . . .' He turned to Professor Rumford
'Professor, you've done a great deal of research on thi
circle, haven't you?'

'I have indeed!' said the old lady proudly.

'You've covered everything? Legends? Folk-lore
History?'

The old lady drew herself up. 'I assure you Doctor
nobody has ever had occasion to question the qualit·
of my research.'

'No, no, of course not,' said the Doctor soothingly
'Where do you keep your notes, if I may ask?'

'Back at Miss Fay's cottage. It's quite close, we'r·
using it as a base for our survey.'

The Doctor nodded. 'Would you be kind enough t·
show your notes to Romana?'

'I'd be only too delighted.'

'Splendid. Perhaps you'll go with the Professor then
Romana?'

'And where are you going?'

'I'm going to see Mr De Vries.'

'What? After what he tried to do to you?'

'Because of what he tried to do to me,' corrected the Doctor. 'He failed, remember? I think Mr De Vries must be a worried man by now, and worried men often sing worried songs. Come on, K9!'

The Doctor hurried off into the darkness, K9 gliding after him.

'All right, girls,' said Professor Rumford briskly. 'Everyone back to the cottage. I've got a lot of research to show you, Romana.' She picked up her old bike from its resting place against the monolith. 'Just hop on the back, there' a good girl.'

Romana looked at the contraption dubiously. 'Would you mind if I just walked?'

'Nonsense, up you get.'

Miss Fay smiled. 'It'll be a new experience for you, won't it, my dear? No need to be afraid!'

Spurred on by Miss Fay's mocking smile, Romana climbed on the back of the bike.

Professor Rumford shoved off, and they wobbled slowly away, down the path.

Miss Fay looked after them, still smiling.

As the Doctor had predicted, De Vries was a very worried man. He was on his knee before the altar in his house beseeching for the mercy of the Cailleach. Mercy, as he knew all too well, was a quality in which the Cailleach was somewhat deficient. She would have little mercy for a servant who had failed her.

De Vries abased himself before the altar. 'O Cailleach, Cailleach ... Great Goddess, have mercy on your poor servant.'

To Martha, the High Priestess, De Vries seemed to have lapsed into a state of terrified hysteria. She herself was more concerned with evading the Earthly authorities than with escaping from supernatural vengeance. The Druids had been little more than a kind of game for her, and now the game was very definitely over.

She shook the terrified man by the shoulder, 'Let's just get away from here. Let's just get in the car and drive off. We can be in Plymouth in a few hours.'

'Plymouth?' moaned De Vries. 'You just don't understand, do you? The Cailleach will find us wherever we go!'

'Why should she follow us? You've always served her loyally in the past. You can't be blamed for just one failure.' Martha shuddered. 'Besides, it's all gone too far. I mean it's one thing sacrificing chickens or even sheep—but human sacrifice!'

'I failed—don't you understand,' screamed De Vries. 'I failed! There's no forgiveness for failure ...' He pointed a quivering finger at the wrought-iron stand. 'Where's the bird?'

'It was here ... it must have just flown away.'

'She summoned it. Her servant has gone ... it's too late, too late ...' De Vries broke into his anguished

52

chant. 'Cailleach, great Goddess, have mercy, have mercy ...'

Suddenly Martha screamed. 'What's that?'

A heavy crunching sound was approaching the house, as if some unbelievably enormous creature was lumbering slowly towards them.

'It's too late,' whispered De Vries. 'Get out, Martha. Get out as fast as you can!'

Martha clutched his arm. 'No, I won't leave you!'

There was a grinding crash as something huge smashed down the front door.

The Doctor and K9 came up to the gates of the gloomy old house. The gate was open and lights were burning on the ground floor.

Suddenly K9 stopped dead. 'Danger, Master. Unidentified alien beings.'

There was a loud shattering crash. A terrified scream echoed into silence.

'Come on K9!' shouted the Doctor. He ran up the front drive.

The heavy oaken front door of De Vries's house was smashed to matchwood. A trail of devastation led down the hall towards the altar room.

Two dead bodies lay at the foot of the stairs, crushed and almost unrecognisable.

Sombrely, the Doctor studied the remains of Martha and De Vries. 'Smashed to pieces,' he murmured. 'Poor De Vries. So much for the rewards of serving the Cailleach.'

There were streaks of some greyish powdery sub
stance across the floor, K9 was snuffling inquisitivel
at them.

'What is it, K9?'

'This is silicon, Master. Whatever attacked thes
two humans left a trail. It leads through here.'

K9 glided towards the altar room.

'Steady, K9, wait for me!' called the Doctor.

The altar room too was wrecked, the furnitur
smashed to fragments. The French windows stoo
open and the curtains waved gently in the nigh
breeze.

K9 glided in, the Doctor close behind him.

The Doctor looked round. 'All clear, K9?'

'Negative, Master. Sensors indicate——'

There was a fierce grinding sound and an enormou
shape loomed up at the window, huge and grey, ye
lit from within by a fiery glow.

The shape surged forward, shattering the window
The Doctor staggered back, throwing up his arm t
protect his face from the shower of glass.

He tripped and fell and as the shape surged afte
him, K9 extruded his blaster and fired.

There was a roar of pain, the glow faded, the creatur
lumbered away. Like a terrier after an elephant, K
glided in pursuit.

The Doctor picked himself up, brushing off frag
ments of broken glass, and looked round dazedly. 'K9
where are you? Come back K9!' He ran through th
French windows and out into the darkness.

Miss Fay's cottage was a cosy, old-fashioned sort of place, the traditional English country cottage with whitewashed walls, low ceilings, chintz curtains and comfortable old-fashioned furniture.

Romana was sitting at a polished oak table going through the notes compiled by Professor Rumford during her exhaustively detailed research. As the old lady had boasted to the Doctor, nothing had been omitted. The results of her labours filled several bulging cardboard folders and a number of equally crammed box-files. Romana was still working her way steadily through the immense mass of material when Professor Rumford came in from the tiny kitchen, bearing two steaming mugs of tea.

She handed one to Romana. 'There you are, my girl. Vivien's in the kitchen, making some sausage sandwiches. Nothing like sausage sandwiches to stimulate the brain! Now then, how are you getting on? Any problems with the notes?'

'No, no, they're very full!' Romana studied a file. 'You say here that you've identified the Nine Travellers, our Stone Circle as one of the Three Gorsedds of Prophecy. What's a Gorsedd?'

'Old Welsh, my dear girl. A Gorsedd is a Place of Augurs—and Augurs are people who can foretell the future. There's an ancient Welsh poem about it—you'll find it in the notes somewhere.'

Miss Fay came in, bearing a plate piled high with sausage sandwiches. She began speaking in a kind of chant, obviously reciting from some ancient text. 'The

Three Gorsedds in the Isle of Britain are: the Gorsedd of Salisbury in England ...'

'That's Stonehenge, of course,' whispered Professor Rumford.

'... The Gorsedd of Bryn Gwyddon in Wales,' Miss Fay paused, '... and the Gorsedd of Boscombe Moor in Damnonium.'

Professor Rumford nudged Romana. 'And that's our Nine Travellers!'

Romana leafed through the notes, 'Why should this particular Circle became a place of prophecy? You say here yourself, there are dozens of Circles in this part of the country.'

Professor Rumford reached for a sausage sandwich. 'If I knew that, my girl, I'd be Professor of Megalithic Archaeology, and not that fool Idwal Morgan.'

'Something else strikes me as curious,' said Romana slowly.

Miss Fay looked up. 'What?'

'Until recently, the land the circle stands on has always been owned by a woman. Have you noticed? Lady Montcalm, Mrs Trefusis, Senhora Camara ... Even back in the middle ages it was under the control of the Mother Superior of the Little Sisters of St Gudula.'

Miss Fay shrugged. 'What does that prove? Lots of convents owned land in the middle ages.'

'It's odd, though, isn't it? It was always women who owned the Circle. All women.'

'What are you suggesting, Romana?' Miss Fay gave one of her faintly scornful smiles. 'Some kind of sisterhood that's been worshipping those Stones ever since the convent was founded in the twelfth century? A cult going back over seven hundred years! That's rather hard to believe, isn't it?'

'What other explanation is there?'

'What about De Vries? He doesn't exactly qualify as the head of a sisterhood!'

'Then maybe he isn't the real head,' said Romana steadily. She turned to Professor Rumford. 'This convent—does it still exist?'

'Good heavens no. And it was a man who saw to that! Henry VIII closed it down during the Dissolution of the Monasteries.'

'What happened to the convent records?'

'I should imagine they were all destroyed,' said Miss Fay carelessly.

Professor Rumford took another swig of tea. 'I suppose so ... though some of them could be still at the Hall.'

'What Hall?'

'De Vries's house. It was built on the site of the convent.'

'Well, let's go and take a look, then,' said Romana. She stood up, scattering papers. 'Come on, what are we waiting for?'

Professor Rumford jumped up too. 'Good girl,' she said approvingly. 'That's the spirit I like. No time like the present, eh? But you've got to eat something first!'

To appease her, Romana managed to force down a few mouthfuls of sausage sandwich and a swig or two of the tea, though it wasn't exactly the kind of food she'd been used to on Gallifrey.

Professor Rumford was rummaging in her desk. Eventually she produced a large and fearsome club.

'What's that?'

'A policeman's truncheon,' said Miss Fay. 'When she went to lecture in New York, she took it with her in case she got mugged.'

'And did she?'

Miss Fay smiled, 'No, she got arrested for carrying an offensive weapon!'

Professor Rumford tucked the truncheon under her arm, 'I'll just get my bike. Coming Vivien?'

'No, you don't need me. Romana can borrow my bicycle.'

'Jolly good. You stay here and keep in a good fire, just in case the Doctor gets back first. Come along, Romana. Tally Ho!'

Exuberantly, Professor Rumford swept Romana out.

Miss Fay sat gazing into the fire, that faintly mocking smile still on her face.

6

The Cailleach

Romana wobbled across the moor on her borrowed bicycle, struggling to keep up with the madly pedalling Professor. To her vast relief they arrived at the Old Hall at last and dismounted, propping their bikes against the gatepost.

They walked up the front path, to the shattered front door.

Professor Rumford was horrified. 'Great Scot, what's happened here? What could possibly have done this?'

Romana made no attempt to answer. Cautiously, they moved through the shattered hall and along to the wrecked altar room. They found the Doctor just inside the french windows, kneeling over the battered body of K9.

Romana hurried forward, 'Doctor are you all right? What's happened to K9?'

Briefly the Doctor explained what had happened. 'K9 drove the thing off,' he concluded. 'There's no doubt about it, he saved my life. Unfortunately, he was rash enough to go chasing off after it—and as you can see, he caught it. By the time I arrived, the thing was gone—and poor old K9 was like this.'

'Poor little fellow,' said Professor Rumford sympathetically. 'Is he badly hurt?'

'That's what I'm trying to find out.' The Doctor opened an inspection hatch in the automaton's side, and studied the mass of damaged circuits.

To their astonishment, K9 spoke. In a feeble voice he said, 'Sorry, Master. I tried—but it was too strong.'

'What was it, K9?' asked the Doctor gently.

With a trace of his old self-assurance K9 said, 'Scanners indicate creature silicon based—globulin dependant ...' His voice became feebler. 'Alien entity is possessed of enormous strength. Enormous ...' The voice ran down into silence.

'Will he be all right, Doctor?' whispered Romana.

'I don't know. There's massive damage to his entire circuitry.'

'But it is repairable? It is, isn't it, Doctor?'

Briefly K9 revived, 'Initial damage report suggests negative, Mistress. Advise cannibalisation of my reusable parts.'

'Nonsense, K9,' said the Doctor cheerfully. 'We're not going to turn you into scrap just yet—are we, Romana?'

Romana drew him to one side, 'Doctor, what can we do?'

'His only chance is total circuit regeneration ... and how are we going to do that in time to save him? It might be kinder to remove the cerebral core right now.'

'No! If we do that, he's finished!'

60

'What else can we do?'

'Is your TARDIS fitted with a molecular stabiliser?'

'Yes, of course. All the old type forties are.'

'I thought so . . . There was a lecture recently at the Academy, on the latest techniques for circuitry regeneration. If we link the molecular stabiliser through to K9's circuit frequency modulator—it might stimulate accelerated self-regeneration.'

'Brilliant!'

'Do you really think so, Doctor?'

'Well, pretty ingenious, anyway. It's worth a try.'

'Anything's worth a try,' said Romana fiercely. 'Look at him. He can't last much longer like this—he's on his last legs!'

K9 didn't actually have any legs, but her meaning was clear.

'Right,' said the Doctor. 'You take him back to the TARDIS and get him connected-up. I'll stay here with Professor Rumford and have a look round for those bodies.'

Professor Rumford looked startled. 'Bodies? What bodies?'

'The ones that were here when I arrived—De Vries and that woman helper of his. They're dead, both of them, killed by that creature. By the time I got back here with K9 they'd been spirited away.'

'Why would anyone want to take dead bodies away?'

'I can think of one very unpleasant possibility,' said the Doctor sombrely. You heard what K9 said. The creature that killed them is globulin dependant.'

'What's globulin?' demanded the old lady irritably

'A protein found in blood.'

'What?'

'That's right, Professor. The creature that killed them needs blood to stay alive.'

Two shapeless huddled forms lay on the ground close to the altar stone. They were the bodies of Martha and De Vries, spirited here by the power of the Cailleach

The Cailleach was herself bending over them now a terrifying sight in her bird-mask and feathered cloak She straightened up, and in the taloned claws was a bronze bowl brimming in blood.

'Even in death, you may serve the Cailleach!'

She carried the bronze bowl to one of the monoliths and spilled the blood down the side of the stone column. The blood was absorbed, greedily sucked up by the stone. There was a fierce red glow in the heart of the monolith, and a deep thudding like the pounding of some giant heart.

'Orgi, you shall do my bidding!' hissed the Cailleach. 'Do you hear me, Orgi. Do you hear me?'

The stone glowed brighter. It seemed to shiver and vibrate, and the mighty heartbeat grew louder ...

With a scholar's patience and precision, Professor Rumford was searching through books that lined one wall of the altar room.

The Doctor strode in and said impatiently, 'Anything?'

'I can't find anything earlier than 1700. How did you get on?'

'I've searched the whole house. It's empty! I felt sure she'd be here somewhere.'

'Who?'

'The Cailleach.'

'The Cailleach? The Witch-Hag?' Professor Rumford was incredulous. 'That's only a legend.'

'So was Troy till Professor Schlieman dug it up,' said the Doctor severely. 'I *saw* the Cailleach, here, I tell you, just before I was knocked out.'

The Doctor went over to the windows and stared out into the darkness. 'Morrigu ... Morridwyn ... Call her what you like. In four thousand years I expect she's had quite a few names. But where is she? There are no statues here, no images, no pictures ...' He looked at the blank spaces on the wall. 'Those missing portraits. They must be here somewhere.'

'I don't see why a few paintings are so important.'

'Then why have they been hidden, eh? Tell me that!' The Doctor thought back to his meeting with De Vries in this very room. ' "Beware the raven and the crow," ' he said. ' "They are her servants." ' The Doctor began pacing about the room. 'Birds!' he said explosively. 'Birds!'

Professor Rumford jumped. 'What? Where?'

'Here,' said the Doctor, and ran his hands over a row of birds carved along the edge of the great stone fireplace. He pressed their heads, one by one. A panel beside the fire slid back, revealing a flight of steps.

'Jumping Joshua, a secret passage,' said Professor Rumford.

'Very probably,' agreed the Doctor. 'Come on, let's see what's inside.' He disappeared into the opening and his muffled voice drifted back. 'Mind these stairs, they're a bit steep.' Valiantly, Professor Rumford followed him, and found herself groping along a narrow passageway.

She heard the Doctor's voice from somewhere ahead of her in the darkness . . . 'Careful Professor.' She heard a muffled thump, and the Doctor said, 'Ouch! You haven't got any kind of light have you.'

'Sorry, Doctor.'

The Doctor felt his way. 'It seems to lead into some kind of secret room . . .'

Professor Rumford groped along the walls. To her astonishment her hand encountered a light-switch, so she switched it on.

She and the Doctor stood blinking in a small square chamber, arched entrances on either side. One dim bulb swung from a flex in the ceiling.

There were pictures hanging on the walls, and the Doctor moved to study the inscriptions beneath them. He paused before the picture of a tall, dark, striking woman in eighteenth-century dress. 'Lady Montcalm, painted by Allan Ramsey.' There were two more pictures hanging beside the first. 'Here we have Mrs Trefusis,' said the Doctor, like a guide at an art gallery. 'And here is Senhora Camara.'

Professor Rumford screwed up her eyes in the dim light. 'They all look familiar ... I seem to know their faces.'

'So you should, Professor. All three of these women have the same face. That of your friend, Miss Vivien Fay!'

Romana stepped back from the TARDIS console and looked worriedly at K9. He was connected to the molecular stabiliser, which was humming with muted power.

This was one of the most advanced techniques of Time Lord technology—a way for a damaged machine to renew and repair itself in the same way as a living creature. But the method was new, experimental. There was no guarantee that it would work.

She went outside, closing the door behind her. She heard a rustle of feathers above her head and looked up. Three black crows were perching on the top of the TARDIS. Romana looked at them uneasily, shivered and hurried away.

She set off across the moor, hurrying as quickly as she could in the darkness. She was well on the way to Miss Fay's cottage when she saw a strange eerie glow in the darkness ahead of her. It was coming from the direction of the Circle of Stones.

Afraid, yet somehow fascinated, Romana changed direction and headed towards the circle.

When she was closer she paused, straining her eyes

to peer ahead. A strange formless glow was coming from the centre of the Circle of Stones, and a deep throbbing note, like the humming of a giant spinning top.

A hand came out of the darkness and gripped her arm. Romana jumped and almost screamed. Standing very close to her in the darkness was Miss Fay. She was wearing a hooded black cloak, a great jewelled pendant, and carried a tall, strangely-shaped staff.

Romana gave a gasp of relief. 'Oh, it's you! You scared the life out of me!'

'Did I? I'm so sorry.'

'There's something strange going on in the Circle!'

'Something strange?' repeated Miss Fay. 'Let's take a look, shall we?'

Still holding Romana's arm, she tugged her towards the Circle. Romana tried to pull free, but Miss Fay was astonishingly strong. She dragged Romana across the moor and into the centre of the Circle, which seemed lit by a strange phosphorescent glow, as though the very ground had become somehow luminous.

'What are you doing?' protested Romana. 'Let go, you're hurting me!'

Miss Fay released her, at the same time giving her a shove that sent her staggering into the exact centre of the glowing Circle.

The deep humming note was very loud now.

'What's going on?' shouted Romana. 'What are you doing?' Miss Fay threw back her head and gave a great peal of terrifying, mad, laughter.

She touched her jewelled pendant, raised her staff

and pointed it at Romana.

A cone of light appeared in the centre of the circle. It spun around Romana like a whirlpool, moving faster and faster until it spun itself into nothingness.

When the whirlpool of light disappeared, Romana had vanished with it.

7

The Vanished

'You know,' said Professor Rumford thoughtfully, 'Vivien Fay never told me she was related to the Montcalm family.'

'She isn't related to the Montcalm family, my dear Professor—she *is* the Montcalm family. And the Trefusis and Camara family as well. And I don't doubt that she's in charge of the company that owns the circle today. These are all portraits of the same person.'

'But look at the dates under the paintings. Look at the costumes. These pictures cover a span of over a hundred and fifty years.'

'What's a hundred and fifty years when you've been around for more than four thousand? Your friend Miss Fay is the Cailleach!'

There was a grinding roar, and they both whirled round. A great, grey glowing shape had appeared at the far end of the passage. It began advancing towards them at an incredible rate. Professor Rumford stood transfixed. The Doctor grabbed her arm. 'Run!' he yelled. They both turned and fled through the other passage.

The thing rumbled after them like a living avalanche, smashing through the arches in its progress.

They sprinted desperately down a corridor, and to their enormous relief, found a flight of steps and a door at the far end. It gave on to the garden, and soon they were running across the garden and down the path to the front gate.

They paused by the gate so that Professor Rumford could catch her breath. 'I never thought we'd get out of that house alive.'

'Well, we're not clear yet! We'd better get on as soon as we can.' The Doctor closed the heavy iron gates behind them.

Professor Rumford couldn't believe what she had seen. 'Doctor, do I understand you correctly—that thing is made of stone?'

'That's right. Fascinating, I know. But may I remind you it's catching up on us fast.'

'But that's impossible.'

'Oh no it isn't. The thing's still moving, and we happen to be standing still!'

'No, no, Doctor, what I meant is that a silicon-based life form is unheard of. It's absolutely unknown— quite impossible!'

There was a roar from close behind them.

'Maybe it doesn't know that?' suggested the Doctor. 'Come on, Professor, run!'

They ran. Minutes later the great stone shape smashed down the iron gates like tissue paper and rumbled after them.

They stumbled across the moor, the glowing shape never far behind them. 'Doctor,' gasped Professor Rumford.

'Yes, what is it?'

'I think it is our duty to try and capture that creature —in the cause of science, you know!'

'How? I mean, have you got any special plans?'

'We should track it to its lair,' declared Professor Rumford sturdily.

The Doctor sighed, 'In case you hadn't noticed, *i* is tracking *us!*' Even as he spoke, the thing surged up out of the darkness. 'Come on,' yelled the Doctor. 'This way.'

He ran on, almost dragging Professor Rumford behind him.

Although the Doctor was running, he wasn't just fleeing for the sake of it.

He had a plan.

Some time later, the Doctor dragged Professor Rumford to the cliff edge, very close to the point where Romana had gone over.

The old lady looked round. They were on a kind of jutting headland, and the glowing monolith was closing in on them fast. Whichever way they fled, it could move to cut off their escape. 'We're trapped,' she screamed.

The Doctor began taking off his coat, and she stared at him in astonishment. 'I know you've been under a strain, Doctor, but really ...'

The Doctor swished his coat to and fro in front of him and yelled 'Olé.'

He advanced on the monolith.

It rushed at him out of the darkness like a charging

bull. The Doctor wheeled gracefully, the coat fluttering close to the edge of his body. The monster shot past, missed him by inches, and plunged over the edge of the cliff.

There was a massive crash, a series of smaller crashes—then silence.

They peered cautiously over the edge of the cliff. There was nothing to be seen.

'Is it dead, do you suppose, Doctor?'

'How do you kill a stone? Still it may be smashed to bits with any luck. Come on, let's see if we can find its mistress.'

They found the Cailleach at the centre of the Circle of Stones. She was drawing a huge circle around herself with the end of her staff. As the point of the staff touched the ground, it described a fiery ring upon the earth.

The Doctor called, 'No need to wear a mask for us, Miss Fay!'

She pushed the mask away from her face.

'Vivien?' called Miss Rumford. 'What's going on? The Doctor says you're the Cailleach!'

Vivien Fay laughed. There was nothing of the gentle lady about her now, and not much that was human. 'I've been so many things, Amelia dear,' she called mockingly. Her fingers stroked the pendant.

'Well, it's all over now, Miss Fay,' shouted the Doctor.

'Not really, Doctor. You see, I've got Romana.'

'Romana? Where is she?'

'Where you will never be able to find her. She'll be perfectly safe—but only as long as you leave me in peace, Doctor.'

'Ah, but I'm afraid I can't do that Miss Fay. You've got something I need.'

'I wouldn't come too close if I were you, Doctor!'

The Doctor stretched out his hand—and touched a power-charged electric barrier that knocked him off his feet with a massive electric shock. He climbed painfully to his feet.

'Static electric charge, eh, Miss Fay? That's a very primitive kind of forcefield.'

'But effective, Doctor!'

The Doctor rubbed his tingling fingers. 'Yes, very.'

'Now don't worry about Romana, Doctor, she's quite all right. It's yourself you need to worry about.'

'Oh, do I? Why?'

Miss Fay gave a peal of mocking laughter. 'Count the stones, Doctor. Beware the Ogri!'

She twirled her staff around her head and vanished in a vortex of multi-coloured light.

Professor Amelia Rumford shook her head disapprovingly. 'I really wouldn't have thought it of Vivien. Most extraordinary behaviour. I wonder what she meant—about counting the stones.'

The Doctor waved round the circle. 'See for yourself. Three of the Stones are missing.'

'What happened to them?'

'Well, one went over the cliff, remember?'

'You mean that thing that chased us—it was one of the Stones?'

'She called them Ogri,' said the Doctor slowly.

'Ogri?'

'Yes ... Ogri from Ogros—that's their home planet. Somewhere in the Tau Ceti star-system. Repulsive place, Ogros. Covered with great swamps full of amino acids ... primitive protein, which the Ogri feed on by absorption. Hence their need of globulin, the nearest terrestial equivalent of their native food. And hence the blood sacrifices on the stones.'

Professor Rumford listened to this little lecture with understandable astonishment. 'And you say there are three of these things?'

'Well, two at least. One down and two to go. Gog and Magog—the ogres. They can't be far away, either. Tell me, Professor, have you by any chance got any Tritium crystals?'

'What about Vivien Fay, Doctor? What about Romana?'

'Listen Professor,' said the Doctor urgently. 'Just you go back to Miss Fay's cottage and find those Tritium crystals for me. I need to pick up one or two things from my TARDIS.'

'But Doctor, where did they both disappear to? How are we going to find them again?'

'I don't know, Professor, not yet. That's why I need those Tritium crystals. Hurry now, I'll meet you at the cottage.'

The Doctor disappeared. Professor Rumford stood for a moment, shaking her grey head in puzzlement.

Then, bracing herself to her duty, she set off for Vivien Fay's cottage.

Later that night, the sitting room of the cottage presented a busy scene. The Doctor had cleared Professor Rumford's notes from the table, and piled it high with an astonishing assortment of electronic circuitry. From this collection he was building a kind of tripod-mounted gun with a cone-shaped muzzle.

K9, still a little shaky but almost himself again, was standing by. To the Doctor's delight, when he had returned to the TARDIS he had found that the molecular regeneration process had succeeded splendidly. By now K9 was almost his old self again.

Professor Rumford came bustling in, holding in her hand a strangely-shaped phial of faintly glowing crystals. 'Are these any good Doctor? The only crystals I could find apart from a packet of Epsom Salts!'

The Doctor opened the phial and peered inside it, 'Well done! I knew she must have some somewhere. It's the only way she could possibly power that wand of hers.'

The Doctor began pouring the crystals into a specially designed storage compartment in the base of his device.

'I still don't understand where Romana and Vivien are, Doctor.'

The Doctor was concentrating on his task. 'I think they're in hyperspace.'

'Hyperspace?'

Suddenly K9 activated himself. 'Hyperspace is an exception to the special theory of relativity proposed by Earth scientist Einstein. This theory states—'

'Don't strain yourself, K9,' interrupted the Doctor. 'You're not fully recovered yet, you know.'

'Circuitry regeneration seventy-five per cent completed, Master,' said K9 proudly.

'Well stop showing off! Didn't I give you some calculations to do?'

'Calculations cannot be completed until device is finally constructed.'

'All right, all right! Then why don't you stop interrupting and let me get on with it? He's a terrible chatterbox once he gets going, you know, Professor.'

Professor Rumford shook her head despairingly. 'I still don't understand about hyperspace.'

The Doctor was cross-connecting a maze of delicate circuitry. 'Who does?'

'*I* do,' said K9 importantly.

'Oh shut up, K9. It's all a matter of interspatial geometry, you see, Professor.'

'Oh dear, I'm afraid I never studied that!'

'I'm not surprised. They gave up teaching it two thousand years ago, even on Gallifrey.' He sighed. 'Let me see, how can I explain. You know Einstein's special Theory of Relativity ...'

'I think I do,' said Professor Rumford proudly. She closed her eyes like a child reciting in class. 'It said you can't travel faster than the speed of light or you'd encounter the Time Distortion effect. In fact you'd reach your destination before you left your starting point!'

'Well, that's more or less right,' said the Doctor generously. 'I always thought it sounded rather fun, myself. I tried to explain about hyperspace to poor old Albert, but he would insist he knew best.' The Doctor drew a deep breath. 'Anyway, apart from things like the space time continuum, and spacewarps, there is also a theory that there exists another *kind* of space.'

'In other words, hyperspace?'

'Exactly, Professor.'

'I still don't see where Vivien and Romana *are*.'

'They're still in the Circle. Or rather, in whatever occupies that space in another dimension.'

'I see,' said Professor Rumford slowly.

The Doctor grinned. 'Splendid. Perhaps you'd explain it to me sometime, when you've got a few minutes to spare?'

He went on with his work.

Professor Rumford cleared her throat. 'May I ask you a rather personal question?'

'Well you can always ask ...'

'I've been noticing one or two things and—well, are you from outer space?'

'No. I'm more from what you might call Inner Time,' said the Doctor solemnly.

'Ah!'

The Doctor stood up and stepped back to admire his work. 'Well, what about that then, K9?'

K9 raised his head and scanned the device, 'An

ingenious construction, Doctor.'

'I know that—but will it work?'

'Affirmative. However, it will be effective only on a setting of .0037 on the hyperspace scale.'

'What? *Only* on that end of the scale?'

'Affirmative, Master.'

'That means it will burn out its circuits in about ten seconds flat!'

K9 whirred and clicked. 'Correction, Master. Circuits will burn out after thirty-one point two-seven seconds of use.'

'And will that be long enough to get me into hyperspace?'

'Insufficient data, Master. Answer depends on where you arrive in hyperspace, and what is there when you arrive.'

The Doctor sighed. 'Thank's very much!'

'Actual transportation area will be small,' warned K9. 'It is imperative, therefore, that you make your point of entry into hyperspace on arrival, to facilitate your return.'

'A good point, K9,' said the Doctor solemnly. He picked up the device. 'Come on, Amelia, I shall need your help. Let's go back to the Circle of Stones, and see if this thing works!'

8

The Prison Ship

The Doctor was setting up his device close to the spot in the Circle of Stones where they had seen Miss Fay disappear. It was very late and very dark now, with black clouds covering the moon. Chill night winds howled eerily across the moor.

The Doctor adjusted the device to his satisfaction and stepped back. 'Now, Professor, do you understand what you have to do?'

'I think so,' she studied the controls. 'I switch on *here*, wait till *this* needle registers 0037 on *this* dial, and throw *that* lever.'

The Doctor nodded approvingly, 'Very good, Professor. But do remember, you've only got about thirty seconds to switch on and then switch off again—otherwise, pow!'

'Pow?' repeated Professor Rumford nervously.

'Yes, pow! That's a technical expression meaning all the micro-circuitry will fuse into one steaming great lump of molten metal!'

'What happens if the Ogri come back when you're still—wherever you'll be?'

'That's where K9 comes in. He'll generate a force-field—one a touch more sophisticated than Miss Fay's.

It ought to keep them out, for a while at least.'

'How long is a while?'

K9 answered for himself, 'In my present state of repair my power-packs will be drained in seventeen minutes thirty-one point thirty-eight seconds at force-field operation.'

'And what about you, Doctor?'

'Don't you worry about me, Amelia, I'll be doing quite enough worrying for both of us!'

'How will you get back?'

'All you have to do is make sure you switch on for not more than thirty seconds, about every half hour. If Romana and I can find our way to our entry-point at a time when you're transmitting, we'll automatically be brought back here, you see?'

It was clear to Professor Rumford that the whole scheme was fraught with danger, for herself and K9, but most of all for the Doctor. 'Well, if you really think it will work . . .'

'Of course it will work. Anyway, even if it doesn't you know what they say about hyperspace?'

'No, what?'

'It's a theoretical absurdity. I've always wanted to be lost in one of those! Now then, are you ready?'

Professor Rumford nodded.

The Doctor took his place in front of the device. 'Right, then. Now!'

Professor Rumford obeyed her instruction with meticulous care. She switched on. She waited till the needle reached 0037. She pulled the lever.

There was a flash of light and a puff of smoke from

79

the device. 'Switch off—quick!' yelled the Doctor.

Professor Rumford switched off, 'Did I do something wrong?'

'You are not to blame,' said K9 consolingly. 'The Doctor has made an error in the circuitry!'

'We're not all programmed for perfection, you know,' said the Doctor crossly.

He came round the back of the machine, fished out a jeweller's eyeglass and his sonic screwdriver, and began repairing the circuitry. 'Ah, there's the trouble! Won't take long to fix.'

'Ogri approaching from the south, Master,' announced K9.

Professor Rumford peered worriedly into the darkness surrounding the Circle of Stones. 'I can't see anything.'

'Second Ogri approaching from the south-west.'

The Doctor worked more quickly, 'Nearly finished. There, that ought to do it.'

He ran round to the front of the device. 'Right, let's hope it works this time.'

'Ogri fifty metres and closing.'

'Now remember, Professor,' said the Doctor urgently. 'Just do exactly as you did before!'

'Very well, Doctor. Are you ready?'

'Ready!'

'Ogri forty metres and closing.'

Professor Rumford switched on. She watched as the needle crept up to the 0037 reading ...

'Ogri twenty-eight metres and closing.'

The needle reached the mark, and she pulled the lever.

A great beam of light shot from the machine, and surrounded the Doctor in a whirling vortex—just as the attacking Ogri rolled into the circle.

'Now, K9,' yelled Professor Rumford.

K9 hummed and throbbed and the advancing Ogri rebounded from his invisible forcefield.

Professor Rumford switched off the machine, and the whirling vortex of light disappeared. The Doctor had disappeared too.

The vortex disappeared, and the Doctor found himself standing not in the Circle of Stones but in the central corridor of a spaceship. The corridor gave on to the control deck, and judging by its size the spaceship was enormous. It was an extremely complex and sophisticated space cruiser, but it was strangely empty and derelict, drifting stranded in hyperspace like some space-age *Marie Celeste*.

'Romana!' yelled the Doctor. 'Romana!' His voice echoed eerily round the cavernous metal interior of the great ship.

He was about to set off looking for her when he remembered K9's warning. He fished a piece of chalk out of his pocket, and chalked an X on the precise spot where he had arrived. He set off to look for Romana.

*

Romana was shackled to the wall of a bare metal-walled prison cell. Shackled next to her were the skeletal remains of some alien creature. Whatever it was, it had been dead for a very long time.

There was a small window high in the cell door, but because of her position, Romana could see nothing through it but a section of metal wall and ceiling.

Suddenly, a face appeared at the window. It was Vivien Fay. She looked expressionlessly at Romana for a moment, and then moved away before Romana could call out to her. The silence returned.

The Doctor found himself in a broad corridor in the very centre of the ship. It was lined with bolted doors, each with its little window, and suddenly the Doctor realised where he was. He was in a jail—a jail which seemed to take up most of the ship. A prison ship, perhaps . . .

He unbolted a cell door at random and the skeleton of some huge, octopod alien creature tumbled out on him, disintegrating into a pile of bones.

'Sorry, old chap,' said the Doctor sadly, and moved on to another door.

He opened quite a few, finding only the remains of various alien beings, some humanoid, some not, but all very dead. He opened yet another cell, and saw only a shackled skeleton. He was about to close it when he saw something stirring on the other side of the cell. He looked, and saw Romana. She was fast asleep.

'All change at Venus for the Brighton line please,'

said the Doctor cheerfully.

Romana awoke. 'Oh very funny,' she said wearily. 'And where have you been? What's happening? And where am I?'

'Well, in strict order of asking: Busy. Nothing. Hyperspace.'

The Doctor looked at the skeleton, 'Your friend doesn't look too well.' He took out his sonic screwdriver and began freeing Romana from her chains. 'What happened to you?'

'I don't know, not exactly. All I remember is Miss Fay dragging me into the Circle of Stones—then I woke up here. Anyway, what do you mean, in hyperspace. We can't be.'

'Why not?'

'Hyperspace is a theoretical absurdity. Everyone knows that.'

'Ask the people on this ship about that. They've been stranded in it for four thousand years!'

Romana was still arguing as she followed the Doctor from the cell, 'That's ridiculous—'

The Doctor led her towards the flight deck. They went along the corridor in which he'd arrived, then on to the flight deck. The Doctor sat in the pilot's chair, punching up readings on the visual display units.

'Even granting the hyperspace hypothesis,' said Romana. 'How do you decelerate an infinite mass? Anyway, why hasn't this ship been seen from Earth? Where are we?'

The Doctor had succeeded in fathoming out the workings of the alien control console. He punched up a picture on a screen. 'There you are,' he said. 'There's our position.'

The screen showed a sort of diagrammatic representation of the Circle of Stones, with the giant circular form of a spaceship in the middle.

Romana looked at the screen. 'According to this, the ship's hovering just a few feet above the Circle. Why can't it be seen?'

'Because the ship exists in a different kind of space from the Circle,' said the Doctor patiently.

'Not in normal four dimensional space, not even in the space/time continuum the TARDIS uses,' said Romana slowly. 'We're in hyperspace!'

'Yes,' said the Doctor, glad she'd accepted it at last.

'Then why did the ship stop here?'

'Who knows?' The Doctor flicked switches and studied the flow of data across the screens.

'Are you sure this thing's been here for a thousand years, Doctor?'

'I think so. Why?'

'Well, look at this flight deck, look at the controls. They all look—new!'

'Maybe someone's been doing the odd bit of spring-cleaning,' suggested the Doctor absently.

'Viven Fay, for instance?'

'Possibly.' The Doctor pointed to a screen. 'Look, Romana, there's plenty of fuel. And as far as I can tell, the drive is still functional.'

'Maybe the ship ran aground!'

'Aground on what?'

'Maybe there are rocks in hyperspace!'

84

The Doctor stood up. 'We'd better search the ship. The third segment must be on board somewhere. Not to mention your old friend Miss Fay.'

Romana sighed, looking at a screen which seemed to show a kind of chart of the whole ship. 'Looks pretty big, doesn't it? Ah well, where do we start?'

Again and again the two Ogri hurled themselves against K9's forcefield. Again and again, they were thrown back, with grinding roars of anger.

'Power depleted,' reported K9 after the latest attack. 'Cannot maintain forcefield for much longer.'

Professor Rumford was busy with her thirty second transmission. She knew that if the forcefield failed the Ogri would kill them—and the Doctor and Romana would be stranded in the limbo of hyperspace forever.

'Come on, K9,' she said encouragingly. 'Never say die!'

'I will never say die,' repeated K9 obediently. 'But I cannot hold the forcefield for much longer.'

To Professor Rumford's disappointment neither the Doctor nor Romana appeared in the circle. Despondently she switched off. 'No one there yet. I'll try later.' If I'm still alive, she thought.

Suddenly, everything seemed very quiet. The roaring and crackling of the attacking Ogri had faded away.

The glowing shapes were retreating across the moor. 'Look, K9,' she whispered. 'The Ogri are going. They've given up.'

'Assumption incorrect, Mistress. Insufficient data.

The Ogri are going. That is not to say they are giving up.'

K9's voice ran down suddenly like a record played too slow. Professor Rumford knelt beside him. 'K9, are you all right?'

In a deep slurred voice K9 said, 'Power exhausted.'

'Can you re-charge yourself?'

'Affirmative. Given time.' There was a pause and then K9 said slowly, 'Theory: Ogri have also gone to recharge.'

'Recharge? How?'

'With globulin.'

'That means they must find more blood!'

'Affirmative.'

Horrified Professor Rumford whispered, 'That means they've gone to kill someone?'

K9 was too exhausted to reply, but she felt sure his theory was correct.

Two hungry Ogri were roaming the moor in search of victims.

9

The Victims

They weren't very experienced campers. In fact, it was their first time under canvas.

Newly-married, too hard-up to afford a proper holiday, they had bought the little tent and set off for the moors.

Wakened by a strange rumbling noise in the night, the young man crawled out of his sleeping bag and stuck his head out between the flaps of the tent. 'Here, Pat, Pat!' he called.

From inside the tent a sleepy girl's voice called, 'What is it?'

'Come and have a look at this. You won't believe it!'

The girl stuck her head out of the tent and gave a gasp of amazement. 'Where did they come from?'

Two enormous stones were looming over their little tent. The man rubbed his eyes. 'No idea. They weren't there when we put the tent up.'

'Perhaps it's a joke. Maybe someone put them there while we were asleep.'

'How?' asked the man simply. 'They must weigh tons.'

'Maybe they're not real,' said the girl. 'Maybe they're plastic fakes.'

She got out of the tent, walked barefoot across the wet grass and put one hand flat on the stone. 'It's real stone all right.' She tried to take her hand away. It wouldn't move, and she gave a scream of panic.

The man scrambled out of the tent. 'What's the matter?'

'My hand,' she moaned. 'My hand!'

He tried to pull her away from the stone but the hand was fixed immovable.

Suddenly, the stones lit up with an unearthly glow and the girl's hand became the bony hand of a skeleton as the life was sucked from her body.

Terrified the man turned to flee, but the second glowing monolith bore down on him smashing him to the ground. The Ogri had found their food.

The Doctor and Romana were still searching the hyperspace cruiser for the missing third segment— keeping a wary eye out for Vivien Fay.

They opened yet another steel cell, but with no result.

'Do you think there's *anything* alive on this ship?' asked Romana, as she moved the Tracer to and fro without result.

'After four thousand years? I doubt it. Though if there is, it's going to be absolutely furious at the delay!'

The Doctor looked in another cell, saw yet another

alien skeleton in the corner, and moved away.

'You know what Romana? I reckon this must have been a prison ship.'

Romana indicated a cell across the corridor. 'Look at that cell, Doctor.'

'What about it?'

'The door is a different colour—red, when the others are grey. And there's a special seal on the door. Do you think . . .'

The Doctor went over and studied the seal. It was large and red and official looking, and inscribed with numerous alien symbols.

'Maybe it's a first class compartment!'

'What does all that writing say, Doctor?'

'No idea. I can't read the script. It probably says "Do Not Open—Penalty Fifty Pounds".'

He peered in through the cell window.

'Anything in there, Doctor?'

'Can't see.'

'What shall we do then?'

'Open it, of course!' The Doctor broke the seal and opened the door.

He looked inside. 'Nothing,' he said. Two shining silver spheres, the size of footballs, shot out of the cell and floated in mid-air above his head.

'What are those things?' asked Romana in astonishment.

'I've no idea.' The Doctor reached out to touch the nearest sphere. It sizzled angrily and the Doctor snatched away his tingling hand.

'It is not permitted to touch the Megara,' announced

the sphere. It had a thin high voice, like the buzz of some electronic bee.

'I beg your pardon. What's the Megara?'

'We are the Megara,' said the second sphere in a voice much like the first. 'We are justice machines.'

'Both of you?' enquired the Doctor, rather amused by the fussy little beings. 'I shall call you Megara One and Megara Two.' Megara One he noticed was very slightly larger.

'What's a justice machine?' whispered Romana.

'We are the law,' said Megara One.

Megara Two said, 'We are judge, jury and executioner.'

The two Megara spoke sometimes alternately, sometimes together in a kind of chanting chorus.

Megara One said, 'Once we have arrived at our verdict.'

'We execute it,' said Megara Two.

'Without fear or favour.'

'Impartially!'

'Well, it's a great relief to know the law is in such good, er, hands,' said the Doctor hurriedly. 'Now, if you'll excuse us, we have to be going.' He turned to Romana. 'Come on,' he hissed.

'What's the matter?'

'Just keep moving. I didn't like that bit about executioner. We don't know what powers those things may have. Come on!'

They had only gone a few steps along the corridor when both Megara chorused, 'Stop!'

Like a warning-shot, an energy bolt flashed over their heads. They stopped.

'Turn round.'

They turned round.

The Megara glided up to them, hovering overhead.

'Do not move,' warned Megara One.

They stood very still.

'Which of you removed the Great Seals?' demanded Megara Two.

'I did,' said the Doctor humbly. 'I feared for your safety.'

'He meant well,' said Megara One.

Megara Two was not impressed. 'The Law clearly states that no one may remove the Great Seals without authorisation. The penalty is death.' It hovered closer to the Doctor. 'Where is your authorisation?'

'I'm sorry,' said the Doctor humbly. 'I didn't know I needed any. You see I'm a stranger here, and I promise I will never, ever remove any seals ever again without proper authorisation.'

Megara One said, 'Contrition is to be accounted in the accused's favour.'

'Ignorance of the law is not.'

'I will undertake his defence.'

'I think you should advise your client that there is little chance of mercy ...'

While the Megara were happily engaged in this debate, the Doctor and Romana tiptoed down the corridor and disappeared round the corner.

Megara One said, 'I will so advise my client ...' The

sphere spun round. 'My client has gone.'

'Further proof of his guilt,' pointed out Megara Two sharply. 'It is no matter. We shall find him. None can escape the Megara.'

The two shining spheres glided after the Doctor and Romana.

All was quiet outside the Circle of Stones. K9 stood dormant by the base of the Doctor's machine.

Professor Rumford stared out into the darkness, huddled inside her duffle-coat. 'No sign of those creatures. Are you re-charged yet, K9?'

'Negative. Re-charging incomplete. Reminder: it is time to switch on the beam.'

Professor Rumford yawned and switched on the machine. 'At least we haven't got those Ogri breathing down our necks.' The spinning vortex of light appeared but this time there was a figure forming within it.

Professor Rumford stepped forward eagerly—and then froze. The figure was not the Doctor or Romana. It was Miss Fay. 'Vivien!'

Miss Fay stretched out her wand towards the Doctor's machine.

'Do not interfere with the machine,' warned K9. 'If you do I shall be forced to stun you.'

Miss Fay laughed, 'You, you ridiculous automaton? You haven't enough power left to strike a match.'

K9 glided feebly towards Miss Fay, then came to a stop.

She laughed. 'There! You see what I mean?'

Professor Rumford stepped forward. Miss Fay raised her staff warningly. 'Stop Amelia, don't make me kill you!' She pointed the staff at the machine which began to glow.

'No,' shouted Professor Rumford. 'They can't get back if you do that——'

The machine exploded, collapsing in a heap of molten metal.

Miss Fay raised her wand again. 'Ogri come, I command you!'

Two Ogri glided forward from the darkness. This time K9 was powerless to stop them.

They halted one each side of Professor Rumford—and waited.

The Doctor and Romana hurried back to the flight deck corridor.

Romana looked over her shoulder. 'Do you think those things will follow us Doctor?'

'What else do you expect justice machines to do?' He picked up his hat and pulled Romana to stand on the circle with him.

'X marks the spot, Romana,' said the Doctor. 'It's here somewhere. Now where is it. You see the projector Professor Rumford is using has a pretty small spread. If we're not in exactly the right place when she switches on, we'll never get back ...'

Romana pointed. 'There, Doctor!' There was a chalk cross on the floor.

They ran to stand on the spot.

'Come on, Professor,' said the Doctor impatiently
'Come on!'

Nothing happened.

Suddenly there was a shimmering in the air and
just before them a vortex began to form.

'What's happening, Doctor? Are we in the wrong
place?'

Enclosed in the vortex Vivien Fay appeared, flanked
by her two Ogri, the pendant at her throat.

She let out one of her peals of mocking laughter
'Too late, Doctor. I have destroyed your pitiful little
machine. Now you are trapped in hyperspace! Ogri—
destroy them!'

The Ogri advanced.

10

The Trial

The Megara streaked onto the flight deck hovering in mid-air above the group.

'Stop,' they ordered. 'Do not harm our prisoner!'

Miss Fay gave a hiss of alarm. 'Ogri—stop. It is the Megara!' Clearly she knew of the strange beings and their powers.

The Ogri halted their advance.

The Doctor glanced up at the shimmering spheres. 'Friends of yours, Miss Fay?'

'Did you break the seals?'

'Well, yes, I'm afraid I did.'

'Silence,' chorussed the Megara. 'The Doctor is ours. Afterwards you may have him.'

'Oh, please, please,' said the Doctor amiably, 'there's no need to quarrel on my account. I mean, there's no hurry, is there? Sorry to disappoint you, Miss Fay.'

'The prisoner has been tried and sentenced in his absence,' announced the Megara. 'The sentence will now be carried out.'

The Doctor looked alarmed. 'What sentence?'

'The sentence is death. You will be executed immediately.'

'Oh *good*,' said Miss Fay. 'May I watch? You don't mind, do you Doctor?'

'Oh, no, no. I'd hate you to miss my execution.'

To Romana's horror, the Megara bobbed menacingly towards the Doctor. 'Prepare for dissolution.'

The Doctor raised his hand. 'Objection!'

'On what grounds?'

'How can there be a sentence of execution when there hasn't been a trial?'

'There has been a trial.'

'There has?' asked the Doctor in astonishment.

'I defended you,' said Megara One.

Megara Two said, 'And I was judge. You were found guilty.'

'But I wasn't there!'

'Immaterial,' announced Megara Two. 'Your defending counsel was. He spoke most eloquently in your defence.'

The Doctor drew himself up. 'I demand the right to conduct my own defence.'

'Not permitted,' said Megara Two promptly.

'Why not?'

'You are humanoid. Therefore you are quite incapable of appreciating the subtleties of the law.'

'Machine law?'

'Of course. There is no other law.'

'Oh yes there is! Just you listen to me for a minute ...'

Megara One interrupted him. 'As your defending counsel, my advice to you is to submit to immediate

96

execution. So much easier and tidier in the end.'

The Doctor shook his head. 'I wish to appeal against my sentence.'

'There are no grounds for appeal.'

'How do you know? You haven't heard my case yet.'

The Megara buzzed agitatedly to each other and sparks flashed between the twin globes.

Miss Fay stepped forward. 'Your Honours, surely you are not going to allow yourself to be persuaded by this criminal?'

'Who are you?' demanded Megara Two. 'Identify yourself to this Court.'

'I am Vivien Fay——'

'She's the reason we're here at all,' interrupted Romana angrily.

'Is it your contention Vivien Fay broke the seals?'

'No. But what I'm saying is——'

'Your evidence is immaterial,' said Megara Two.

'And incompetent,' added Megara One sternly.

'Attempts to influence the Bench by immaterial means are punishable by death.'

'Article 23 of the Megara Legal Code, sub-section 17!'

The Doctor raised his voice, 'I say, could we get back to the question of my appeal?'

There were more buzzes and clicks and flashes from the Megara.

Then Megara Two announced, 'In accordance with Article 14 of the Legal Code, sub-section 135, the execution of this humanoid will be delayed for two

97

hours, while the Court graciously consents to hear his appeal.'

The Doctor and Romana gave simultaneous sighs of relief.

Megara One rather spoiled things by adding, 'After the appeal has been heard, the execution will take place as ordered!'

The Doctor bowed. 'Your Honours are too kind!'

'I demand that you execute him now!' shouted Miss Fay.

The Megara bobbed towards her.

'Silence!'

'You are out of order!'

'Ha!' said the Doctor and folded his arms with an air of triumph.

Ever since Miss Fay and her Ogri had vanished into hyperspace, Professor Rumford had been kneeling beside K9, trying to revive him.

At last, to her relief, the little automaton's eyes lit up, and his tail antenna wagged feebly. 'Oh thank heavens,' she said. 'Are you feeling better now, poor little chap?'

'Thank you ... Professor Rumford.'

'Can you move?'

'Mobility still somewhat impaired, but data-banks re-charging.'

'What are we going to do? Vivien Fay's wrecked the Doctor's machine and now he's stranded.'

'We shall re-construct the machine. With your help

it will not be too difficult.'

'With my help?' asked Professor Rumford dubiously. 'I'm an archeologist, not an engineer.'

'You are a reasonably intelligent humanoid. You will work under my direction.'

Professor Rumford sighed. 'If you say so, K9.' She picked up the remnants of the machine.

'What about the missing segment of the Key to Time?' asked Romana.

The Doctor shrugged, 'Well, it's here in hyperspace somewhere.'

'We haven't got time for all this trial nonsense. Why don't you tell the Megara about our quest, tell them we're Time Lords.'

'I doubt if they'd listen, Romana. They're justice machines, remember.' The Doctor sighed. 'I heard about a galactic federation once, lots of different life forms. They built an all-powerful justice machine to administer and enforce the law.'

'What happened?'

'It found the Federation in contempt of Court and blew up the Galaxy.'

They were sitting in a corner of the flight deck. The Megara had allowed the Doctor to withdraw to prepare his case. Miss Fay and her Ogri were on the far side of the huge flight deck, waiting impatiently for the Doctor's execution.

Megara Two came bobbing towards them. 'The prisoner will rise.'

The Doctor and Romana stood up.

'The Court has considered the request of the humanoid known as the Doctor. In order to speed up the process of law and the administration of justice it will graciously permit him to conduct his own defence—prior to his execution.'

The Doctor bowed, 'Thank you, your Honours.'

They walked to the centre of the flight deck, and up to the main control console, which the Megara had evidently decided to use as the bench in their improvised courtroom.

'Be seated,' ordered Megara One.

The Doctor and Romana sat in the crew control chairs. Miss Fay came forward to observe the proceedings, long fingers stroking her pendant.

'You may call your first witness,' announced Megara Two.

The Doctor bowed again, 'I call as my first witness, Miss Romanadveratrelundar!'

This was Romana's full Time Lady name. The Doctor thought its use would add a nice touch of formality to the proceedings.

Romana was astonished. 'Me? I'm not a witness.'

'Once you have been called, you must appear. That is the law,' said Megara One.

Megara Two hovered over Romana. 'The witness will take the stand and be sworn in.'

Megara One chanted, 'The witness will take the oath. "I swear to tell the truth ..." repeat the oath.'

'I swear to tell the truth ...'

'"As far as I, a mere humanoid ..."'

Romana looked up indignantly, 'I object to that wording!'

'An objection will be regarded as contempt of Court. Contempt of Court is punishable by death.'

The Doctor jumped up. 'I am sure the witness wishes to withdraw her remark. Don't you?'

'Do you?' asked Megara One.

Romana gritted her teeth and nodded, and went on with the oath. '—As far as I, a mere humanoid ...'

'"Am capable of knowing the truth".'

'... Am capable of knowing the truth.'

Suddenly a long, snake-like metallic flex shot out of Megara Two. It ended in a circlet which clamped itself around Romana's head. She looked up, startled. 'What's that?'

Megara One said, 'It assesses the level of truth.'

'What happens if the level falls too low?'

'That would be most regrettable for you, Miss Romanadveratrelundar. You may begin cross-examining your witness, Doctor.'

The Doctor rose, 'Miss Romanadveratrelundar, when we opened all the other cells here what did we find?'

'Dead things.'

'Expand on that please.'

Romana shrugged. 'Dead things. Bodies, skeletons, bones, mummified corpses. Dead travellers, I suppose.'

'And when we found the compartment in which their Honours,' the Doctor bobbed his head to the hovering globes—'were travelling, could you see what was inside the compartment?'

'No.'

'What did you think was inside?'

'I had no idea. It could have been anything.'

'Even perhaps creatures who had somehow survived?' suggested the Doctor swiftly. 'Creatures still alive, and in need of our help?'

'Yes, of course. That's partly why we broke the seals.'

'No further questions,' said the Doctor and sat down.

'The witness is excused.'

Romana sat down too.

'The Court stands adjourned.'

Professor Rumford completed a circuit connection and looked dubiously at it, 'How's that, K9? Is it all right?'

They were back in Miss Fay's cottage. Before them lay the broken up machine which Miss Fay had destroyed, and a pile of spare parts left over from its original construction.

'Excellent,' said K9. 'You have now linked the Alpha Circuit to the Sine Interphase!'

'I have? Is that right?'

'Affirmative.'

'Oh good. It's not so difficult, after all!'

'Continue. We must hurry. Time is short.'

The brief adjournment was over, and the Doctor was on his feet again. 'Your Honours, I call my second witness—Miss Vivien Fay.'

Miss Fay backed away. 'No, I'm not a witness.'

'That is for their Honours to decide,' said the Doctor swiftly. As he had hoped, the appeal to the vanity of the Megara had its effect.

Megara Two said, 'Once you have been called you must appear. That is the Law.'

For some reason the idea seemed to terrify Miss Fay. 'But I'm not a witness,' she protested. 'I didn't see anything, I don't know anything, Your Honours.'

'You must appear,' repeated Megara Two. 'It is the Law.'

Miss Fay leaped back. 'Ogri!' she screamed.

One of the Ogri lumbered menacingly towards the Megara.

Beams of light surged forth from each of the silver spheres, combined, and struck the Ogri.

There was a blinding flash and it disintegrated.

A small pile of grainy sand was left on the metal floor of the flight deck.

Romana leaned across to the Doctor, 'I see what you mean about that exploding galaxy!'

Megara One hovered over to Miss Fay, 'You will take the oath.'

Miss Fay bowed her head, 'I will take the oath.'

While the oath-taking process was going on, Romana whispered, 'What are you up to, Doctor?'

'I'm trying to find out who Miss Fay really is.'

'Is that important?'

'It could be very important.'

'Why?'

'Because the knowledge could save my life,' said the Doctor. 'And very possibly yours as well!'

11

Surprise Witness

Romana stared at the Doctor in astonishment. 'What do you mean, Doctor? Why should knowing who Miss Fay really is save our lives?'

The Doctor answered her question with another. 'Why do you think the Megara are really here?'

'You think they're after Miss Fay?'

'Well, who else has been hanging about this part of the world for four thousand years?'

'Why don't they arrest her?'

'Maybe because they're justices not policemen. Somehow I've got to bring Miss Fay under the jurisdiction of the Court.'

'I suppose some of those poor creatures we found were police?'

'Yes. It's a pity they're all so dead, isn't it?'

'If this *is* a police vessel, there must be some kind of description of her in their files. A voice print, an encephalographic trace, a retina pattern ... there must be something ...' Romana had a sudden inspiration. 'If I could only get back to her cottage. There must be something incriminating there. Look, Doctor, I've been excused as a witness now. When the trial starts again, I'll slip away and see if I can get back. If K9 and Professor Rumford start transmitting again ...'

'Good girl. It's worth a try.'

'Will you be able to keep things going here?'

'I hope so—but not for very much longer. They're getting impatient!'

As if to reinforce his words Megara One called, 'The witness has taken the oath, Doctor. The Court is waiting.'

The Doctor rose and bowed. 'My apologies to Your Honours. I was just conferring with my associate.'

Romana had already slipped out of her seat and was edging towards the door.

The Megara didn't seem to notice—but Miss Fay did.

'Where is that girl going? She has no right to leave the Court without permission.'

'Irrelevant!' shouted the Doctor. 'What does it matter where she goes? She has given her testimony. None can escape the Megara! Is that not so, Your Honours?'

Again the appeal to vanity had its effect, 'You may proceed with your questioning Doctor.'

The Doctor bowed, and smiled.

His smile faded as Megara Two added, 'Your execution is long overdue.'

By now Romana had slipped away. Miss Fay gestured to the surviving Ogri, and it followed her from the flight deck.

The Doctor looked from the Megara to Miss Fay, waiting for the assessment circlet to be attached to her forehead. To his disappointment, nothing happened.

'I request that this witness be attached to the Truth Assessor.'

'Request denied,' said Megara One impassively. 'It is unnecessary.'

'Why? The previous witness was attached to the Assessor.'

'The previous witness was present when the seals were broken. This witness was not. The Truth Assessor may be used only in the case of vital, direct testimony. Other use contravenes the rights of the witness.'

'I demand that this witness be treated in the same manner as the one before.'

'Demand?' chorused the Megara threateningly.

'Well, request, then.'

'Request denied. Proceed with cross-examination.'

Miss Fay smiled.

On the corridor from the flight deck Romana paced uneasily up and down, taking care to keep close to the Doctor's chalked cross. If Miss Fay hadn't succeeded in destroying the Doctor's machine completely ...

The Ogri glided slowly along the corridor towards her. It seemed to be watching ...

Professor Rumford and K9 were back in the Circle of Stones setting up the re-built machine.

'Perhaps we ought to re-check the wiring,' Professor

Rumford said worriedly. 'Suppose I did something wrong.'

'*I* was supervising,' said K9. 'You did nothing wrong.'

'Just the same . . .'

'Transmit!' ordered K9.

Crossing her fingers, Professor Rumford switched on. The machine began to throb with power . . .

To Romana's delight a spinning vortex of light suddenly appeared over the Doctor's mark. She rushed towards it—and the Ogri rushed towards her . . .

Caught up in the vortex, Romana and Ogri disappeared together——

—and reappeared in the Circle of Stones, beside Professor Rumford and K9.

'Romana,' said Professor Rumford delightedly.

'Look out!' yelled Romana and sprang from the vortex, rolling over and over.

'Danger! Danger! Ogri!' warned K9.

For a moment the Ogri stood motionless, as if confused by the sudden transition from hyperspace.

Professor Rumford snatched up the machine. Followed by Romana and K9 she fled into the darkness.

The Doctor was arguing for his life. 'I suggest, most respectfully, that in this matter, Your Honours are in error.'

'Error is impossible,' said Megara One. 'We are programmed against the possibility of error.'

The Doctor drew a deep breath. 'You have ruled
that the witness, calling herself Miss Fay, need not be
attached to the Truth Assessor because she was not
present when the seals were broken.'

'Correct.'

'How do you know that?'

'We did not see her when we emerged.'

'That isn't proof she wasn't there, though, is it?'

The Megara were rapidly losing patience. 'Do you
say that she was there?'

'I say only that she will never tell anything approaching the truth unless she is forced to. I don't think she'll
even tell us as much as her right name unless she does
so through fear of the Assessor!'

Miss Fay intervened. 'Your Honours, may I humbly
offer a suggestion to resolve this problem.'

'Proceed.'

If it will simplify proceedings, Your Honours, then
let me say I have no objection to submitting to the
Assessor—for the one relevant question. Attach me to
it. Ask if I broke the seals. I will answer that I did not,
and the Assessor will confirm that I speak the truth.
Everything else is irrelevant.'

The Doctor sighed. Miss Fay had out-manoeuvred
him. He went on arguing valiantly, but it was no use.

The silver flex snaked out, and the circlet fastened
onto Miss Fay's head.

'In view of the previous dispute, *I* will conduct your

questioning,' announced Megara Two. 'Are you ready, Miss Fay?'

'Ready Your Honour.'

'You must answer my questions truthfully. Should you lie, the Assessor will register the degree of untruth and react accordingly. Do you understand?'

'I understand, Your Honour.'

'Did you, or did you not remove the seals from the official compartment in which my colleague and I were travelling?'

'I did not.'

'A reading of zero point six on the truth scale,' announced Megara One. 'This is an answer within the legal definition of truth.'

'Are you sure?' demanded the Doctor.

'We do not make mistakes,' chorussed the Megara.

The Doctor exploded. 'How do you know? You were sealed in that compartment for four thousand years. Even the finest piece of machinery degenerates in time. Rust, dirt, pieces of fluff. How would you feel if you condemned some innocent humanoid to death, just because you'd got a bit of fluff caught in your sprocket holes, or whatever you've got in there!'

'We are composed of living cells,' said Megara One. 'We are a microcellular metallic organism. We are bio-machines, incapable of error.'

'Then test yourself,' shouted the Doctor. 'Ask her her real name, I dare you!'

'Irrelevant,' said Megara Two.

'Irrational,' said Megara One. 'Doctor, *you* broke

the seals without official authorisation. The penalty for this offence is execution.'

'I thought you were supposed to be on my side. A fine lawyer you turned out to be!'

'You are my client. I have your interests at heart. I will plead with my colleague for a swift and painless death for you.'

'Plea granted,' said Megara Two instantly.

'You see, Doctor,' said Megara One triumphantly. 'Justice can be merciful! You may step down Miss Fay.'

The circlet unfastened and retracted.

'Thank you, Your Honour,' said Miss Fay sweetly.

The Megara hovered over the Doctor's head. 'We shall now proceed with the execution.'

'Objection!' yelled the Doctor.

There was a note of weariness in the Megara voices. 'What are you objecting to this time?'

'I haven't finished presenting my case. I still have another witness to call.'

Megara One said, 'But there *are* no other witnesses to call. No one else is here.'

'You're wrong, Your Honour. There is one more witness I can call.'

'Who is that?'

The Doctor's finger shot out pointing directly at the hovering sphere.

'You!'

*

K9, Romana and the Professor had just reached Miss Fay's cottage. Professor Rumford put the machine carefully on the table.

'You stay on guard, K9,' ordered Romana. 'Now then Professor Rumford, you've spent a lot of time with Miss Fay. Is there any part of the house where she wouldn't let you go? Any drawers or cupboards she kept locked?'

Professor Rumford thought for a moment, and then shook her head.

'All right,' said Romana. 'Then we'll just have to search at random. We may as well start here.'

Some considerable time later, they were still searching. Books and papers were spread everywhere, and every drawer and cupboard had been turned out.

'It's hopeless,' said Professor Rumford. 'We don't even know what we're looking for. We may already have seen it and not recognised it. It could be at the Hall! Any luck, K9?'

K9 emerged from rooting in a cupboard. 'Negative.'

Romana was leafing through a cookery book. 'A lot of these recipes seemed to have been crossed out ... all the ones containing any form of lemon juice ...'

'Yes, she was allergic to lemon juice,' said Professor Rumford. 'In fact to any kind of citrus fruit—oranges, grapefruit, avocados. Don't see what you're getting at.'

'I wonder why the Ogri never attacked her,' said Romana thoughtfully.

'Maybe they didn't fancy her blood.'

'Precisely. Which may mean that her blood is different from that of humans. K9, what kind of planet produces a metabolism that can't tolerate citric acid?'

K9 whirred and clicked, 'Referring to memory banks Mistress.'

Romana turned to Professor Rumford. 'Is there anything else strange about her you could think of. Anything that might give us a clue?'

K9 gave an electronic bleep. 'Most probable planet of origin G class planet in Tau Ceti. Two other possibilities, but both incapable of supporting human life.'

'Tau Ceti sound the most likely,' agreed Romana. 'And the planet Ogros, where the Ogri come from, is in the same star system!'

The mention of Ogri caused an uncomfortable silence.

'Talking of Ogri,' said Professor Rumford uneasily, 'what happened to our friend out there?'

'We don't know how intelligent it is on its own,' said Romana slowly. 'I suppose it's possible it could track us down though ...'

A grinding rumbling sound came from outside.

'Ogri approaching,' said K9 belatedly. The search had distracted him from his guard duties.

'How close?' asked Romana urgently.

The Ogri came smashing through the cottage window.

12

Verdict

'Quick!' yelled Romana. 'Everyone out of here!'

She snatched up the machine and fled through the door, the others close behind her.

The Ogri was too big to go through the door, and without its mistress it didn't seem to have the sense to crash through as it had in the past. They could hear it still blundering about in the cottage like a great stone bee in a bottle as they fled across the moor.

Once back in the Circle, Romana helped Professor Rumford to set up the machine.

As they worked, Romana muttered, 'Well, at least we can prove she's got a non-terran metabolism. She comes from a G class planet in Tau Ceti. We even know the date of her arrival on Earth.'

Professor Rumford looked up from her work. 'We do?'

'How long has this circle been here?'

'Nearly four thousand years.'

'That's when she arrived.'

'Yes, of course,' said Professor Rumford vaguely. 'Nearly ready, chaps.' The machine was proving a little balky perhaps because of all the carrying to and fro.

'Danger, Ogri,' called K9.

The Ogri had smashed its way out of the cottage. It had crossed the moor, and now it was lumbering up to the edge of the Circle of Stones . . .

K9 promptly projected his forcefield. It was feeble enough, since his re-charging was not complete, but it was enough to slow the Ogri, if not to stop it. The Ogri forced its way forward like a man wading through treacle . . .

'Hurry, Mistress, hurry!' urged K9. 'Speed is imperative. Forcefield will not hold . . .'

The wrangle in the courtroom had been going on for some considerable time.

'We are justice machines,' insisted Megara One. 'We are judge, jury and executioner. We cannot be called to give evidence in our own Court.'

'Why not?' said the Doctor. 'I only want to put my own counsel on the stand. Surely there's no law to say I can't do that? Well—is there?'

Megara Two said unwillingly, 'According to our date banks, the Law does not actually specify that the accused may not call his own counsel . . .'

'There you are then,' said the Doctor triumphantly. 'I call Megara One.'

'Very well,' said Megara Two. 'But it is most unorthodox. Indeed, it may be grounds for a charge of contempt of Court.'

The Doctor was prepared to risk that. He turned to Megara One, who had moved a little apart from his colleague as if in recognition of his new status as a witness. 'I think we can dispense with the oath, Your Honour.'

Megara One was outraged: 'You most certainly can. Megara cannot lie.'

'That's handy ... now then, why were you travelling inside a sealed compartment, with a punishment of death for unauthorised breaking of the seals?'

'To protect us from influence, or contamination, of course. We are justice machines, travelling on judicial business.'

'Travelling to where?'

'Diplos, a G class planet in Tau Ceti.'

'What was the nature of your mission?'

'To preside at the trial of a humanoid criminal.'

'A female humanoid criminal?'

'Correct.'

The Doctor glanced at Miss Fay. 'Of what crime had this female humanoid been accused?'

'Murder. And the removal and misuse of the Great Seal of Diplos.'

The Doctor looked again at Miss Fay—and saw her hand fly to the jewelled pendant about her neck. 'I see. And has the Great Seal of Diplos any special powers?'

'It has the powers of transmutation, transformation, and the establishing of hyperspatial and temporal co-ordinates. The criminal used it to flee from justice.'

'Just as I thought,' said the Doctor happily.

Megara Two intervened. 'Is this relevant?'

'Well it is to me, Your Honour.' The Doctor looked at Megara One. 'What's this female humanoid called?'

'She is known as Cessair of Diplos.'

'And her description?'

'None is available. An officer of the Court was to identify her to us when we reached our destination.'

'But the officers are all dead!'

'That is so.'

'So, you've no way of knowing who she is?' persisted the Doctor.

Miss Fay jumped up. 'All this is irrelevant, Your Honours. The Doctor is simply wasting the time of the Court in order to delay his long-overdue execution.'

'Agreed,' said Megara One.

'Don't you see, *she*'s Cessair of Diplos,' shouted the Doctor. 'She used the Great Seal to escape, stranded you here!'

'Prove it,' taunted Miss Fay.

'Listen to me,' begged the Doctor. 'Why else is she here, in hyperspace? What's the ship doing here?'

Megara Two said. 'That is supposition. Supposition is not proof.'

Miss Fay said confidently. 'I am Vivien Fay of Rose Cottage in Boscawen. Anyone in Boscawen will identify me.'

The Megara floated closer together. 'The proceedings will now be terminated. Prepare to eliminate the accused!' They hovered over to the Doctor.

'Prepare yourself to die, Doctor,' said Megara One.

'Do you usually execute your own clients?'

'We are allowed only to execute prisoners who have been tried and found properly guilty. '

'Well, it certainly adds a new dimension to the role of defending counsel,' said the Doctor bitterly.

The Megara came even closer.

'Wait a minute,' protested the Doctor. 'Aren't you going to offer me a last toffee apple? A bag of jelly babies? A hearty breakfast? A free pardon? Nothing?'

'It is too late, Doctor,' said Megara One, with a tinge of sadness. 'Goodbye!'

A beam of light shot from the Megara to the Doctor and the Doctor leaped at Miss Fay and grabbed her arm.

The fierce light flickered round them both, and they fell to the ground.

Inch by inch, the Ogri had edged closer. Now it was actually within the Circle of Stones, frighteningly close to Romana and Professor Rumford as they struggled with the machine.

'Mistress, speed imperative,' gasped K9. 'I cannot hold him ...'

The machine hummed into life, and Romana leaped into the swirling cone of light. 'Hurry, Professor, hurry! Beam me through.'

The Ogri charged.

The Doctor opened his eyes and saw Megara One hovering close by. Megara Two was hovering over Miss Fay, who lay unconscious, the clamp of the Truth

Assessor attached to her head.

The Doctor sat up groggily. 'What happened? Did I short circuit you?'

'Why did you try to involve Miss Fay in your execution,' demanded Megara One angrily.

'Is she all right?'

'We had no legal authority to kill her, therefore we were forced to cut off the destructive ray,' complained Megara One. 'We are checking for damage.'

Megara Two reported, 'She has not been harmed. She is merely unconscious.'

'Quickly,' said the Doctor urgently. 'Reach into her memory cells!'

'Why should we do that?'

'You might have damaged her brain, mightn't you. It's your duty to make sure it's all right.'

Megara Two buzzed and whirred. A note almost of excitement came into its voice. 'I have reached her memory cells. This humanoid is not called Vivien Fay. She is Cessair of Diplos. She is guilty of the theft and misuse of the Great Seal of Diplos.' More buzzes and clicks. 'She is also guilty of removing the two silicon-based life forms from the planet Ogros, in contravention of article 7954 of the Galactic Charter, and of employing them for criminal ends.'

The Doctor heaved a great sigh of relief. 'You see? All you had to do was look into her memory cells!'

Megara One said defensively, 'According to Article 3, Section 185 of the Galactic Code, it is not permissible for Megara to read the memory cells of any beings unless they are unable to present their evidence by reason of death, unconsciousness or natural stupidity.'

The Truth Assessor unfastened and retracted, and Miss Fay opened her eyes and looked round dazedly.

At the same moment, Romana came hurtling onto the flight deck. 'Stop,' she shouted. 'I've brought new evidence!'

The Doctor grinned, 'Too late, I've just been executed!'

Romana stared at him, 'What?'

'By the way,' added the Doctor. 'Did you know there was an Ogri just behind you?'

Romana spun round. The Ogri was lumbering remorselessly down the corridor after her. 'Oh no! Professor Rumford must have beamed it through by accident.'

The Ogri trundled menacingly towards them.

Megara One snapped, 'Ogri, stop! We are the Megara. We command you to stop!'

The Ogri stopped, like a well-trained dog.

Vivien Fay was awake and on her feet by now, gazing wildly around her, unable to grasp how things had gone so suddenly wrong for her. 'What's happening?' she cried. 'Ogri!'

Remembering, perhaps, what had happened to its fellow, the Ogri did not move.

Megara One said severely, 'Ogri you will be confined to a suitable cell on this vessel until you can be returned to your home planet.'

The hovering spheres converged on Vivien Fay. 'Cessair of Diplos,' said Megara Two severely, 'you have been tried and found guilty of the following charges: illegal detention of this vessel in hyperspace, for which the penalty is death, or imprisonment for one thousand years. Impersonating a religious personage, to wit a celtic goddess, for which the penalty is imprisonment for one thousand five hundred years. Theft of the Great Seal of Diplos, for which the penalty is perpetual imprisonment. The sentences will run concurrently. Have you anything to say?'

Cessair of Diplos, sometimes known as the Cailleach, also known as Lady Montcalm, Senhora Camara, Mrs Trefausis, and Miss Vivien Fay stared at her captors in bitter silence.

Professor Rumford was watching the dawn rise over the Circle of Stones, the faithful K9 at her feet. She had almost given up hope of ever seeing the Doctor and Romana again, when they suddenly materialised before her in a vortex of light. Vivien Fay was with them too, as well as two silvery globes that hung buzzing in mid air in the most astonishing fashion. 'Doctor! Romana! Vivien!' cried Professor Rumford, as if counting them off. She peered bemusedly at the hovering spheres. 'What are those things?'

The Doctor gave her a hug. 'Those, Professor, are the Megara, they're justice machines, and they're about to carry out sentence.' He drew her to one side. 'I'd stand well back if I were you.'

Miss Fay stood in the centre of the Circle of Stones. She raised her head and looked at the Doctor, her eyes filled with hatred. 'If you let them do this to me, Doctor, you'll never find what you're looking for!'

'Oh, I wouldn't go so far as that. Excuse me gentlemen, I think this is mine.' Before anyone could stop him, the Doctor sprang forward with surprising speed and lifted the great jewelled pendant from around Vivien Fay's neck. 'I think this is what I need.' He backed away and stood beside the others.

'Sentence will be carried out,' said the Megara.

Miss Vivien Fay backed away, back and back until she was standing in a gap between two of the remaining monoliths. She seemed to freeze, her body shimmered ... and she became a monolith herself, another stone standing between the others.

'Perpetual imprisonment,' chanted the Megara eerily. 'Sentence has been executed.'

The Doctor looked up at the Megara as they hovered in the centre of the Circle, their silver bodies reflecting the dawn sunshine. 'Well gentlemen, I think that concludes your business?'

Megara One said, 'Not quite, Doctor.'

'There is still the matter of your interrupted execution,' said Megara Two. 'We shall carry it out here and now.'

The Doctor shook his head in astonishment at their persistence. 'I really don't think we need bother with that!' He swung the glittering pendant in his hand. 'Safe journey, gentlemen!'

The Megara vanished.

'Where are they going?' asked Romana.

'Back to Diplos. I took the liberty of pre-setting the

controls on their ship before we popped back down here. That should give me a few thousand years of grace, I hope! Well, come along, we can't hang around here any longer, we've got work to do.' Tucking his machine under his arm he led Romana and K9 towards the TARDIS.

Professor Rumford took one last look at the stone that had once been Vivien Fay and followed him.

As they walked up to the TARDIS she was saying 'Poor Vivien, I can't help feeling sorry for her. And she hasn't finished making trouble yet, I'm afraid.'

'What do you mean?' asked Romana, with an apprehensive glance behind her.

'Well, the Nine Travellers, my dear. Three gone because they were really those Ogri things, then one replaced by poor Vivien ... they'll have to call them the Seven Travellers now. And they'll all have to be surveyed again. It's going to put the cat among the archaeological pigeons and no mistake!'

The Doctor paused by the TARDIS and fished out his key. 'Never mind, Professor. Think what a monograph you'll be able to write about it!'

Amelia Rumford chuckled. 'Yes, it'll make Idwal Morris look an absolute idiot.'

'Will you put in *everything* that's happened?' asked Romana mischievously.

'Certainly not! I do have my academic reputation to consider.' Professor Rumford saw the Doctor was opening the door of the police box. 'That's funny. I never knew there was a police box there before ...'

She was even more surprised when K9 glided inside the police box.

Romana gave her a kiss on the cheek. 'Goodbye, Professor, thank you for everything.'

The Doctor came forward and gave her a hug. 'Goodbye Amelia. Take care!'

He followed the others inside the police box and closed the door.

'Goodbye?' said Professor Rumford. 'Where do they think they're going in a police box?'

She got her answer a few minutes later when the police box produced the most astonishing, wheezing groaning sound, and faded away.

Professor Amelia Rumford scratched her head. 'Better keep very quiet about this, Amelia my girl,' she told herself sternly. 'You do have your academic reputation to consider!' She stumped away to begin her survey of the Circle of Stones.

The Doctor stood by the TARDIS console swinging Vivien Fay's pendant in his hand. 'Well, that was all most satisfactory! I'd like to have seen poor Amelia's face when we dematerialised.'

'Doctor, is Earth always like that?' asked Romana wonderingly.

'No, no, Earth's a very varied planet. Sometimes it can be quite exciting! Pass me the Tracer, will you?'

Romana handed it to him.

The Doctor put the pendant down on the console

and touched it with the Tracer. The pendant shimmered and turned into an oddly-shaped piece of crystal.

The Doctor picked up the fragment of crystal, went over to the wall-safe and opened it with his palm-print. He took the large, irregularly shaped chunk of crystal from inside and compared it with the small irregularly shaped piece of crystal in his other hand. He tried to fit them together. He couldn't do it.

Romana watched his efforts for a moment. She went over to him and took the fragments of crystal from him. She studied them for a moment, fitted them together, and the two pieces of crystal merged into one.

Another segment of the Key to Time had been found.

But there was still a fourth, a fifth, a sixth ...

The TARDIS sped on its way, taking the Doctor, Romana and K9 to new adventures, in their quest to save the cosmos from the power of chaos.

'Doctor Who'

Δ	0426114558	Terrance Dicks **DOCTOR WHO AND THE ABOMINABLE SNOWMEN**	70p
Δ	0426200373	Terrance Dicks **DOCTOR WHO AND THE ANDROID INVASION**	60p
Δ	0426116313	Ian Marter **DOCTOR WHO AND THE ARK IN SPACE**	70p
Δ	0426116747	Terrance Dicks **DOCTOR WHO AND THE BRAIN OF MORBIUS**	60p
Δ	0426110250	Terrance Dicks **DOCTOR WHO AND THE CARNIVAL OF MONSTERS**	70p
Δ	042611471X	Malcolm Hulke **DOCTOR WHO AND THE CAVE-MONSTERS**	70p
Δ	0426117034	Terrance Dicks **DOCTOR WHO AND THE CLAWS OF AXOS**	70p
Δ	0426113160	David Whitaker **DOCTOR WHO AND THE CRUSADERS**	70p
Δ	0426114981	Brian Hayles **DOCTOR WHO AND THE CURSE OF PELADON**	70p
Δ	042611244X	Terrance Dicks **DOCTOR WHO AND THE DALEK INVASION OF EARTH**	70p
Δ	0426103807	Terrance Dicks **DOCTOR WHO AND THE DAY OF THE DALEKS**	70p
Δ	0426101103	David Whitaker **DOCTOR WHO AND THE DALEKS**	70p
Δ	0426119657	Terrance Dicks **DOCTOR WHO AND THE DEADLY ASSASSIN**	60p
Δ	0426200063	Terrance Dicks **DOCTOR WHO AND THE FACE OF EVIL**	70p
Δ	0426112601	Terrance Dicks **DOCTOR WHO AND THE GENESIS OF THE DALEKS**	60p

†For sale in Britain and Ireland only.
*Not for sale in Canada.
♦ Film & T.V. tie-ins.

†For sale in Britain and Ireland only.
*Not for sale in Canada.
♦ Film & T.V. tie-ins.

Δ	0426112792	Terrance Dicks **DOCTOR WHO AND THE GIANT ROBOT**	70p
Δ	0426115430	Malcolm Hulke **DOCTOR WHO AND THE GREEN DEATH**	60p
Δ	0426200330	Terrance Dicks **DOCTOR WHO AND THE HAND OF FEAR**	60p
Δ	0426200098	Terrance Dicks **DOCTOR WHO AND THE HORROR OF FANG ROCK**	70p
Δ	0426200772	Terrance Dicks **DOCTOR WHO AND THE IMAGE OF THE FENDAHL**	70p
Δ	0426200543	Terrance Dicks **DOCTOR WHO AND THE INVISIBLE ENEMY**	60p
	0426200039	**DOCTOR WHO DISCOVERS SPACE TRAVEL (NF) (illus)**	75p
	0426200047	**DOCTOR WHO DISCOVERS STRANGE AND MYSTERIOUS CREATURES (NF) (illus)**	75p
	042620008X	**DOCTOR WHO DISCOVERS THE STORY OF EARLY MAN (NF) (illus)**	75p
	0426200136	**DOCTOR WHO DISCOVERS THE CONQUERORS (NF) (illus)**	75p

†For sale in Britain and Ireland only.
*Not for sale in Canada.
♦ Film & T.V. tie-ins.

If you enjoyed this book and would like to have information sent to you about other TARGET titles, write to the address below.

You will also receive:
A FREE TARGET BADGE!
Based on the TARGET BOOKS symbol — see front cover of this book — this attractive three-colour badge, pinned to your blazer-lapel or jumper, will excite the interest and comment of all your friends!

and you will be further entitled to:
FREE ENTRY INTO THE TARGET DRAW!
All you have to do is cut off the coupon below, write on it your name and address in *block capitals,* and pin it to your letter. Twice a year, in June, and December, coupons will be drawn 'from the hat' and the winner will receive a complete year's set of TARGET books.

Write to:

TARGET BOOKS
44 Hill Street
London W1X 8LB

cut here

Full name ....

Address..

....

....

Age.....................

PLEASE ENCLOSE A SELF-ADDRESSED STAMPED ENVELOPE WITH YOUR COUPON!